W.I.T.C.H.

Will   Irma   Taranee   Cornelia   Hay Lin

The Last Tear

Adapted by ELIZABETH LENHARD

HYPERION/ DISNEY
New York

© 2004 Disney Enterprises, Inc.

W.I.T.C.H. Will Irma Taranee Cornelia Hay Lin is a trademark of Disney Enterprises, Inc.
The Volo colophon is a trademark of Disney Enterprises, Inc.
Volo® is a registered trademark of Disney Enterprises, Inc.

Printed in the United States of America
First Edition
1 3 5 7 9 10 8 6 4 2

This book is set in 12/16.5 Hiroshige Book.
ISBN 0-7868-1732-1
Visit www.clubwitch.com

IT MOVES IN THE DARK.
MASTER OF THE DARKNESS, IT RUNS IN THE SHADOWS QUICKLY AND QUIETLY.
IT BREATHES SHARPLY. IT TURNS. IT JUMPS. IT ESCAPES.
ITS HEART BEATS WILDLY. IT HEARS STEPS GETTING CLOSER. IT KNOWS IT IS IN A TRAP. . . .
. . . AND WHAT IS WORSE IS THAT SHE KNOWS IT, TOO.
COME ON, GET OUT FROM THERE! YOU'RE IN BIG TROUBLE THIS TIME!
GNIK!

HELLO? HI, I WAS LOOKING FOR MATT.... I AM A FRIEND. AH...AND WHERE MAY I FIND HIM? IT'S KIND OF URGENT.

I'LL WRITE IT DOWN. ALMOND STREET...

AT NUMBER 12 ALMOND STREET

MATT'S GRANDFATHER'S PET SHOP!

M—MAY... MAY I COME IN?

COME IN, MISS. WHAT CAN I DO FOR YOU?

AH, IT'S YOU!

UM... HELLO, MATT.

OH! DO YOU TWO KNOW EACH OTHER?

HAVE YOU COME TO SLAP ME AGAIN, OR IS THIS A COURTESY VISIT?

I...I CAN EXPLAIN EVERY-THING.

HMPH! GO ON AND TALK AS IF I WERE NOT HERE!

ENCHANTED TO MEET YOU, MISS . . .

WILL! WILL VANDOM!

AND THIS IS YOUR DORMOUSE. THEY AREN'T REALLY PETS. . . .

WILL ALREADY SAVED HIM ONCE—AT THE PARK, A WHILE AGO.

WELL DONE, YOUNG LADY. AND SOMETHING TELLS ME THAT THIS LITTLE BEAST WILL BE OKAY. YOU MUST BE ITS GUARDIAN ANGEL!

IF YOU DON'T MIND, I'D LIKE TO KEEP IT HERE UNDER OBSERVATION. IN TWO DAYS YOU SHOULD BE ABLE TO TAKE IT BACK HOME.

WOW! IT'S A KIND OF ANIMAL HOSPITAL!

MY GRANDFATHER HAS BEEN WORKING AS A VETERINARY SURGEON FOR ABOUT FIFTY YEARS.

AND I JUST CANNOT STOP, TO TELL YOU THE TRUTH . . .

GRANDPA ONLY SELLS HIS ANIMALS TO PEOPLE HE LIKES!

YOU BET! THAT'S WHY I DON'T SELL MANY OF THEM! I HAVE PECULIAR TASTES. I . . .

ONE

Irma Lair gaped at her mother.

As usual, Mrs. Lair had her fists planted on her hips, and she was glaring at her daughter.

Also as usual, Irma was responding with a glare of her own. Irma didn't have to look at a mirror to know which expression she was wearing. It was her tried-and-true Mask of Horror, with added touches of incredulity and scorn. It was tailor-made for Mom.

It was also the only expression Irma could muster at that particularly terrible moment.

My mother, Irma thought desperately, has just ordered me to do the unthinkable. She is making me leave my cozy, quiet bedroom. . . .

Here, Irma paused and looked around her bedroom. Okay, so it wasn't *exactly* quiet, what

with the stereo blaring and her pet turtle, Leafy, loudly gnawing on a carrot in his bowl. And cozy? Well, if you call a heap of somewhat fragrant laundry on the floor and a vanity table piled high with unfinished homework cozy, then cozy was exactly what Irma's room was.

The point, Irma thought with a shrug, is that my mother is *throwing* me out of the sanctuary of our home. She's making me go . . . on a date!

Irma realized immediately that this sounded odd. After all, she was a normal teenage girl. She went to school. She loved shopping, body-surfing at the beach, talking to her girlfriends on the phone, *and* dating. I like dating boys—cute, sporty, *stylish* ones, Irma thought. This date is with a total nerd! He is, in fact, the most unbearable dweeb at the Sheffield Institute—the skinny, bespectacled Martin Tubbs!

"Irma," Mom scolded. She stepped through Irma's bedroom door threateningly. "You promised!"

"Promised?" Irma squeaked. "When would I have promised anything like that?"

"Irma!" Mom repeated. Her blue eyes narrowed to slits and her forehead scrunched into a field of angry furrows. "If you don't leave this bedroom immediately, I will get very, very angry."

Irma looked around her bedroom desperately. Her eyes fell on the stack of schoolbooks lying on top of her vanity table. Homework! Homework trumped everything! Irma dived toward the desk and scooped up a couple of textbooks.

"I want to do my homework!" she wailed. "I have to study. Send Leafy instead of me!" Irma pointed to her pet turtle.

"Your turtle is not going on a date with Martin Tubbs!" Mom sputtered. "*You* are! Now come on! You're acting like a little girl!"

Mom grabbed Irma by the wrist and began dragging her into the hallway.

This is child abuse! Irma thought. But she knew not to play that card with her mom, who, after all, was *usually* quite the softie. She was always baking cookies and helping Irma and her brother, Christopher, with their homework and stuff like that.

That's it! Irma thought suddenly. I'll appeal to Mom's soft side.

"A mother cannot do this to her favorite daughter," she cried, grabbing on to the door as

Mom tried to yank her down the stairs.

"You're my *only* daughter," Mom pointed out, through gritted teeth.

"Don't you have a heart?" Irma wailed. In a tragic gesture, Irma lifted her own hand to her chest. She gazed beseechingly at her Mom and let her lower lip tremble, just a bit.

"Please," Mom said, rolling her eyes.

Hey! Irma thought indignantly. That eye roll is *my* move! No fair!

"Don't make such a stink," Mom continued. "You made the date. And now, you'll keep it."

Mom grabbed Irma by both shoulders and began to march her down the stairs toward the living room. Irma sighed heavily. She was beaten. There was no getting out of it. And the worst part of this grievous miscarriage of justice? Irma really *hadn't* made the date.

It was my stupid astral drop who said yes when Martin asked her out, Irma thought with a groan.

Ah, the good old astral drop, she mused grumpily. She's been the *most* inconvenient part of being a Guardian of the Veil. Well, that and being attacked by slimy, scaly monsters every time I turn around.

Lately, Irma's normal, teenage life had been . . . not so normal after all.

Things had first started getting weird while Irma was soaking in a long, hot bath one day. She'd been lazily trailing her fingers through the steamy bathwater as she daydreamed about her fave TV show, *Boy Comet*. Then, suddenly, Irma had noticed something bizarre! In her fingers' wake, the bathwater had begun to do more than simply ripple and undulate. It had started floating! Big blobs of water had risen from the water and danced before Irma's incredulous eyes.

Then, with a flick of her finger, Irma had sent the water soaring around the bathroom like a fleet of flying saucers!

Over the next few days, Irma had discovered that she could coax ocean waves to crash where she wanted; convince great geysers to rise out of the earth; even redirect rain!

And that wasn't all. Irma had also found she could predict pop-quiz questions, simply by making a wish.

Meanwhile, her best friends at school—Cornelia, Hay Lin, Taranee, and Will—had all started experiencing supernatural and bizarre moments of their own.

Before any of them had had a chance to *really* freak out about their strange new powers, Hay Lin's mysterious grandmother had filled them in on their new situation: beings in a heavenly place called Candracar had anointed the five girls to, well, save the world.

Yeah, Irma thought drily, *then* it was time to freak out. First of all, we learned that we all had magical powers and that Will held the key to those powers. She's the keeper of the Heart of Candracar, this glowy, crystal orb that pops out of her palm every now and again. Every time she unleashes that glowing orb, we all turn into superbeings! We get to wear really cool outfits. Oh, yeah, we can also control all the elements. I'll manipulate anything wet and watery. Hay Lin is all about air. Taranee lassos fire. And Cornelia can control the earth. *That* one makes perfect sense, since Cornelia's such a stick-in-the-mud.

Irma giggled at her joke, even if it had only been in her head. Sure, she loved Cornelia—she'd known her a long time. But even when they were younger, Cornelia had been a little uptight.

A *little* uptight? Irma thought with a roll of the eyes. Who am I kidding? She's a total control freak! Of all us Guardians, *she's* been the most resistant to this whole we're-magic-and-we-have-to-save-the-world thing.

Of course, Irma thought ruefully as she plodded down the stairs, we were *all* a little resistant to our next discovery. And that was? Basically, that we—we earthlings—are definitely not alone. In fact, there are a whole bunch of other worlds floating around out there. One of those worlds is Metamoor.

Irma shuddered at the very thought of Metamoor—a dusky, Gothic-looking place inhabited by talking lizards, leering, blue thugs, and a ruthless hunter named Frost. Metamoor was a dark land of exile—a place that had been taken over by evil.

That was why the all-knowing Oracle of Candracar had created the Veil. The Veil was a barrier that separated Metamoor and earth. For centuries, the Veil had stood stalwart, and no one ever crossed the supernatural fence.

But when the most recent millennium had hit, the Veil had become weak and porous. In twelve spots, the Veil had been punctured completely, creating portals between earth and Metamoor. All of those gateways just happened to be located in Heatherfield, otherwise known as Irma's very own hometown. Put simply—it was the young Guardians' job to find the portals and seal them.

Simple, but not easy!

Hay Lin's grandmother had given the girls a guide to the portals. But the magical map only revealed each opening's location *after* it had been found.

What's more, the Guardians usually found a portal just as some evil monster came through it, itching for a fight! The girls had already battled a few Metamoorian goons, and barely escaped with their lives.

Almost as soon as the Guardians had been handed their mission, their friend, Elyon Brown, had traveled through a portal, never to return. She'd totally defected to Metamoor. She'd also turned cold and evil. Now she was trying to coerce the Guardians into joining her.

Talk about a catfight, Irma thought, as she landed at the bottom of the stairs.

Elyon had tried all sorts of dirty tricks to sway her friends. She'd teased and tormented them. Then she'd almost killed them, with the help of some predatory, writhing, brick walls.

Finally, she'd kidnapped Taranee and tricked her into believing her friends had forgotten her.

Elyon's mistake had been in underestimating the Guardians. They'd rushed to Metamoor to rescue Taranee. The mission was dangerous, and the Guardians had had no idea how long they'd be gone. So, right before they'd left, they'd used their magic to create astral drops: magical doubles who stood in for the girls at school and home. The scheme had pretty much worked! Not one of the girls' parents had detected their absence. Irma's double had even taken a science test for her!

But then again, her astral drop had also agreed to go on a date with Martin Tubbs!

My astral drop was supposed to absorb everything bouncing around in my brain, Irma thought in despair. And mostly, she got it right. When I came back to earth and absorbed her experiences, I found that she'd talked back in gym class when the coach tried to make her serve the volleyball. *So* me! I hate serving! She also shunned Mom's gross turkey meat loaf and took a two-hour bath. So she *must* have known how much I loathed Martin. I've loathed him since we were practically toddlers. Nobody with any common sense would ever agree to a date with . . .

Martin! As Irma stalked into the living room, she spotted him, sitting in the overstuffed chair. Christopher, her annoying little brother, was sitting nearby, playing a video game on TV. When Irma walked into the room, Christopher gave her a teasing sneer.

"Don't you say a word," Irma muttered.

Irma sized Martin up immediately, from his flushed face and Coke-bottle glasses to his horrendous outfit! He was wearing his goofy, blue Explorer Scout uniform—shorts, dark socks, and neckerchief! Awkwardly, Martin scuttled out of his chair and waved at Irma. He gave her a googly-eyed grin.

"Say hello to your friend, Irma," Mom said, with a stern look.

"My little doughnut!" Martin cried, rushing across the room to Irma. "You look simply ravishing."

Irma closed her eyes, swallowed hard, and counted backward from ten. It was going to be a *long* afternoon!

TWO

Martin could not believe his luck! He, yes, he—Martin Tubbs, who only yesterday had been humiliatingly given a wedgie by one of Sheffield Institute's many bullies—was about to go on a date with Irma Lair. *The* Irma Lair.

As he hurried across the room toward his beloved, Martin skimmed over his hair with one hand. He'd experimented with some styling mousse that morning, spending about half an hour arranging the straw-colored strands to match a picture he'd found in an old copy of *Lion Beat* magazine.

Yes, yes, very fashionable, Martin thought as his fingers brushed over the crusty helmet of hair. Irma will love it! At least, that's what I figured out last night from the book I just bought, *Dating for Smarties*.

In his head, Martin quoted from Chapter 7: *Do not, under any circumstances, show up for your date in your same old brown, corduroy pants and* Star Journey *convention T-shirt. Show your lady that you have put some effort into your appearance. Buy yourself some new threads, and make sure you shave.*

Martin didn't have to worry about shaving yet. But he *had* given his outfit hours of thought. And he thought his selection was *pret*-ty dazzling, if he did say so himsel—

"What's *up* with the outfit, Martin?" Irma cried, piercing Martin's self-appraisal with her usual, er, wit. "Are you auditioning for the circus? Or did your closet explode, leaving you with *nothing* to wear except your . . . Explorer Scouts uniform?"

Irma's big eyes—as blue as the *ocean*, Martin thought—focused on Martin's crisp uniform for a moment before quickly shifting away.

"It's my Sunday best!" Martin told Irma, laughing off her insult as he usually did. He *knew* she was just teasing him . . . uh, as she usually did. But just in case, Martin was mindful of Chapter 11 of *Dating for Smarties*: "Don't be the strong and silent type," the author had admonished. "Girls like a modern man, who can share their emotions. About *her*, that is. No gushing on about the miracle that is your new, 120-megahertz Pentium hard drive, beautiful as it may be!"

Right, Martin thought. Expressing emotions. The *perfect* way to start a first date! Here goes!

"You see, Irma," Martin expressed. "I chose these fancy threads because this is an amazing opportunity. I've been waiting for this moment for years. Going out with you is my life's dream!"

Irma rolled her eyes.

"You know, that's a coincidence," she snapped. "Going out with you is *my* nightmare. So, let's make it snappy, okay? Where do I have to go with you?"

As Irma slipped her arms into a pink hoodie, her mother stepped forward and squeezed her daughter's shoulder—and squeezed it hard, from the looks of her white knuckles.

"Please excuse her, Martin," Mom said over Irma's head. "She must have woken up on the wrong side of the bed. She's usually quite kind."

Martin nodded and smiled politely. As he did, he felt a familiar pain—a pang, actually—smack in the middle of his chest. Why was he sensing this old sting? Because Irma was acting like the old Irma again—the one who had rejected him each of the 736 times he'd asked her out before. The one who had put him into a headlock every morning throughout the third grade and demanded his milk money. The one who . . . didn't want to be caught dead with him in public.

Could it be, Martin thought, that the Irma who agreed to go out with me was some sort of impostor? Like the cyborg doppelgänger who invaded the spaceship in *Star Journey*, episode number forty-seven?

Martin shrugged and smiled.

Nah! he thought. That kind of thing only happens in television shows and stuff! Now, it *is* possible Irma had the flu when she said yes! But no matter. Now that I've got her all to myself, I'll have a chance to impress her. By the end of this date, she'll be *captivated*. She will be my date to the spring prom! And she will beat up any bully who tries to give me a wedgie, from this day forward!

Completely cheered, Martin walked to the front door. And he willfully pretended not to hear when Irma hissed to her mother, "How can I be kind when he's dressed that way?!"

Martin wiped the sweat off his palm to open the door. When he stepped outside, Irma actually followed him! This date was going great! His seductive skills had even gotten the attention of Irma's little brother, Christopher, who had abandoned his video game to watch the teenagers leave. Having an audience had given Martin an extra bolt of confidence.

"All the girls talk like this at first," he told Irma as they headed down the walk. "But you're underestimating me, my little sweet potato. Behind this face lurks a sensitive creature."

Irma gaped at Martin. Then she looked away.

Martin hoped mentioning his face hadn't called attention to the big zit on his nose.

Irma did not even look at him again. She stomped toward the street, but not before Christopher had called out a squeaky-voiced good-bye: "Have fun, my little sweet potato!"

"Grrrrr," Irma snarled. Sending Martin a

loathing-filled look, she turned right and began hightailing it down the street.

"You read my mind," Martin panted as he hurried after her. "I'm taking you out to the Heatherfield Museum. I already have tickets. We Explorer Scouts get special discounts!"

Martin waited for Irma's reaction. Would she like his idea? Girls like Irma often preferred the mall, but Martin was *much* more knowledgeable about dinosaur bones and medieval manuscripts than he was about frozen yogurt flavors and the latest in denim washes. He wanted to impress Irma with his smarts!

When Irma nodded in brusque agreement and continued walking in the direction of the museum, Martin felt a thrill.

Score! he thought. One point for Martin Tubbs.

Martin glanced at his watch. Uh-oh. It had been about four minutes and twenty-five seconds since he'd expressed any emotion. Better get on the ball if he was going to make Irma fall in love with him by curfew!

"Irma?" he said. He winced as his voice cracked, but pressed on. "I don't want to get too mushy, but I really believe we're made for each other. Sure, you look at me now, in this official-looking uniform, and you think I'm a real straight arrow. But that isn't the real me."

"Oh, I know it," Irma said. She turned a corner and headed for a flight of stone steps. The museum was just a few blocks away. "The real you is a lot worse."

"Irma!" Martin giggled. "What I mean is, there's untapped strength in me. I look like this now. But I could change in an instant if I just, say, took off my glasses."

Martin swiped his glasses off his nose and squinted at her. Irma's beautiful, if surly face, suddenly went fuzzy. Martin could barely see his beloved! But it was worth the sacrifice. He needed Irma to see the real him—the dashing man behind the glasses. If only she would stop walking and look at him! No matter—Martin could talk and walk—well, stumble—at the same time.

"See, look at me now," he said, puffing out his chest. "Don't I look like—*aaaaigggggh!*"

Ba-dump, ba-damp, thud, thud, skiidddddd.

Ooooooh, Martin groaned a moment later. Wha—what happened?

Turning his head painfully to one side, he

found himself nose-to-cement with the bottom step of a flight of stairs. The last time he had been able to see, Martin had been at the *top* of those stairs.

Martin groaned again and closed his eyes. *Owwwww!* He was bruised and battered. Nothing could possibly cure his painnnn—

"Martin!"

Martin's eyes popped open! Never mind! The concern in Irma's shrill voice made him completely forget his almost-broken bones.

Now, Irma's hazy face appeared above him. Sighing, she reached down and placed his glasses on his face. As she came into focus, Martin saw her bite her lip. Her forehead was furrowed with concern and—wait a minute— Martin had never seen that look on Irma's face before. Was it guilt?

From his position flat on his back, Martin winked at his date.

"So," he said to her. "Who do I look like without my glasses?"

Irma heaved a deep sigh.

"A goof," she said softly. "You look like a nearsighted goof, Martin." But the surly edge had left her voice.

Here's the part where she declares her love for me! Martin thought hopefully.

But alas, before Irma could form the words, an elderly lady appeared at the kids' side, offering to call an ambulance. Martin waved her off gallantly.

"Don't you worry, ma'am," he said, jumping to his feet and brushing off his skinned knees. "Everything's under control!"

Noting with another inward thrill Irma's raised eyebrows, Martin resumed his walk toward the museum. Irma fell into step beside him. And this time, she didn't dart ahead, or stomp. She simply walked.

Soon, the pair were climbing the museum's grand, marble staircase.

"Here we are," Martin announced happily. "The Heatherfield Museum. One day, we'll be laughing together, and we'll say, 'Remember that afternoon, after school, when we went to the Heatherfield Museum?' I can just see it."

"Martin," Irma said. She bit her lip again, took a deep breath, and plunged ahead. This looked serious!

"Martin," she said again quietly. "You're a good friend—a pain in the neck—but a friend.

Only a friend. Do you understand? That I'm here with you today, but only in friendship? You have to open your eyes to that."

"I do?" Martin asked.

"It would be better for everybody," Irma said, placing one hand gently on Martin's shoulder. "Believe me."

"O—okay," Martin said.

The warmth and weight of Irma's hand on his shoulder had an unexpected effect on Martin. He'd always thought that Irma's touch would send zings of happiness thrumming through his heart. But instead, he found himself feeling . . . a sense of peace!

He supposed he'd always known that such a conversation would happen. He'd just never expected Irma to be so wistful about it. Or so nice! Maybe this *would* be the start of a beautiful friendship. And shockingly, Martin thought, maybe that would be enough for him.

Feeling a new lightness—and less nervousness—in his footsteps, Martin took a deep breath and smiled.

"I *have* been a fool," he admitted. "I guess you want to head home now?"

"Not at all," Irma said with a smile. "You've

dragged me to the museum. Let's go see it"

"Aha!" Martin cried. "See? Deep down, your heart belongs to me. I know it."

"Martin . . ." Irma said. But she laughed lightly as they walked into the museum. For once, they both got the joke. Martin happily steered Irma away from the museum's art gallery and into the natural history department.

"Let's go here, my little pancake," he said. "We can start with the dinosaurs. Because that's where humanity started, after all. We're all descended from these big, scaly creatures."

"Gee, the first date and you're already introducing me to the family?" Irma quipped drily. "I guess you *are* serious."

Martin pointed up at a giant brontosaurus skeleton. The big, craggy skull seemed to be peering right at them.

"Raise your voice a bit," Martin said, glancing away from Irma's smiling face to gaze at the skeleton. "You know, Grandma's kind of deaf."

Eeeeeeeeeekkkkk!

"Aaiighhh!" Martin cried, clapping his hands over his ears and turning back to Irma in shock. He liked Irma's drama queen ways, but this was out of control. "I'd say that's raising your voice a little too much, Irma."

"That wasn't me!" she exclaimed.

But the scream had definitely come from another girl nearby! The sound was so terrifying, Martin's first impulse was to flee. He assumed Irma would be right there next to him.

This afternoon was full of surprises. When Martin looked at Irma, she didn't look freaked at all. In fact, she looked curious—eager, even, to find the source of that scream. Before Martin knew it, Irma had begun dashing out of the dinosaur exhibit—and toward the woman's scream. With a bewildered shrug, Martin set out after her.

They reached the gallery exit just in time to see a woman in a blue suit dashing into the museum's foyer. Still screaming, she headed straight for the protective arms of a security guard.

"Miss Stevens!" the guard exclaimed in a panic. "What's wrong?"

Wait a minute, Martin thought in alarm. That woman is in uniform. *She*'s a security guard, too! If a *guard* is this freaked out, something must be really wrong.

"Over there," Miss Stevens stammered,

pointing down a gloomy hallway toward a small art gallery. "Over th—there. It's horrible!"

As Miss Stevens continued to cling to the man, he unhooked a walkie-talkie from his belt.

"Command?" he blurted out. "Emergency on the east side!"

Irma grabbed Martin's jacket sleeve.

"Let's go see!" she whispered. Martin gaped at her in disbelief.

"Are you serious?" he squeaked.

When Irma nodded, Martin shrugged his skinny shoulders and acquiesced.

"Wow," he muttered. "I knew a date with Irma Lair would be unforgettable, but I had no idea it would turn into some kind of action-adventure movie! I just want to know one thing—when do I get to yell, 'Cut'?"

THREE

As Irma led Martin into the gallery, she could only imagine his confusion. First she'd gone all nice on him—a phenomenon that Irma *herself* was still trying to wrap her brain around. And now, she was doing this hero thing. She knew it must have seemed majorly out of character.

Only a short time ago, it *would* have been, Irma thought. But now that I'm a Guardian, it feels as if Superhero is my middle name.

Irma snuck down the dusky hallway with Martin in tow. When they arrived in the small, shadowy gallery, she shuddered. It was eerily quiet. Figures from the looming oil paintings on the walls seemed to leer out at the kids.

Martin crowded behind Irma and whispered, "I don't see anything."

Kssssssssshhhhhhh!

Irma gulped. Slowly she glanced up at a corner of the gallery. Sure enough, she spotted a
ghastly creature—a giant, yellow-eyed, hissing
lizard, dressed in a brown, suede tunic!

I'd recognize that Metamoorian fashion
faux pas anywhere, Irma thought. One of the
bad guys has come to pay another call on
earth. Just dandy!

"Uh, Martin," Irma said quietly. "If you look
harder, you *will* see something."

Martin looked harder.

Then he jumped about a foot in the air.

And *then* he cried, "Holy smokes! Let's get
out of here!"

Martin darted out of the gallery, shrieking
all the way.

Irma stood her ground. She'd battled creatures a lot meaner and scarier than this
ol' reptile. She wasn't terribly worried. But she
did want to know what the reptile was doing
hanging around the Heatherfield Museum.

Apparently, the curiosity was mutual. The
slimy visitor skittered down the gallery wall and
crept toward Irma on all fours. Then it rose up
on its hind legs and flicked its forked tongue in
her direction. Irma's lip curled as she took a

deep breath, but she didn't back down.

Let it try something, she thought bravely. In two seconds flat, I could whip up a supersized water balloon with that lizard's name on it!

Sniiffff, ssssssssniiiffff.

The lizard cocked its slick head at Irma—and spoke!

"You are . . ." it hissed.

Suddenly, the lizard's yellow eyes bulged in surprise. "A Guardian! *Hiisssssssss!* A *Guardian*!"

Before Irma could reply, the frightened creature whipped around. In fact, it turned so fast it almost tripped Irma with its ten-foot-long tail. It scrambled back up the wall, ducking into the gloom of the gallery's darkest corner.

"Wait!" Irma cried desperately. "Don't go away! Hold on!"

But the lizard didn't look back. In an instant it completely disappeared into the shadows of the gallery.

Where'd it go? Irma thought in bewilderment. It's like it just melted into nothing. She stared up at the now-empty corner for a moment.

Anxiety began to gnaw at her gut. It was becoming painfully clear that the Guardians' work would never be done. Every time Irma began to relax—to get back into the routine of her old life of school, mall trips, and gossip sessions with her friends—some new crisis seemed to rear its ugly head.

Or its ugly, giant lizard's head!

Irma was just starting to freak out when she was startled by the sound of feet pounding behind her. When she glanced over her shoulder, she saw Martin and two burly, armed guards hurrying into the gallery.

"Everything okay, miss?" one guard asked.

"Huh?" Irma said vaguely. She glanced back up at the shady corner. The lizard had definitely disappeared. "Oh, uh, sure, officer."

Miss Stevens, the guard who had been so terrified, crept into the gallery.

"But, there was a creature here," she insisted. "It jumped out of thin air!"

"I saw it, too," Martin whispered. "Did you? It was some kind of giant reptile! Maybe one of the dinosaur eggs finally hatched!"

Oh, my friend, Irma thought wearily. If only it were that simple!

FOUR

Hay Lin tried to take a deep breath. It was a struggle. The air this morning felt so heavy. It was oppressive . . . practically unbreathable!

And the reasons for that are what? Hay Lin wondered drily. Well, the simplest answer would be that it's pouring.

She gazed out of the covered walkway where she was hanging with her friends. Just beyond their narrow shelter—one of many open-air corridors that linked the various buildings of the Sheffield Institute—the schoolyard was positively soaked. The sky was gray and rumbled with thunder. The rain was coming down so hard that small swimming pools were forming on the lawn. Hay Lin even thought for a minute that she saw a bird doing the backstroke in one of them!

But, gee, rainy weather? thought Hay Lin with a frown. That's too easy an explanation. I know the real reason my lungs feel as if they were filled with cotton. It's because these days, I'm painfully aware of—well, the air! After all, I'm Breezy Girl—the Guardian with the power over the wind. Hay Lin couldn't help but laugh as she imagined herself jetting about on frothy gusts of air. The pizzicato giggle seemed to grab hold of her long, black pigtails, making them swoop upward and dance around her ears. Hay Lin grabbed her glossy tresses and smoothed them down. She glanced around to make sure nobody had glimpsed that magic moment. Luckily, all the other Sheffielders were occupied with dodging raindrops or trekking to class.

Somehow, I don't think the other students would get this whole "air goddess" thing, Hay Lin thought. Except for my fellow Guardians, of course.

She cast a grateful glance at her tight little circle of friends—Will, Irma, Cornelia, and Taranee. Without them in on the secret, this Guardian stuff would be no fun!

And let's face it, Hay Lin thought with a

sigh. Even *with* my friends at my side, being a Guardian isn't much fun these days.

That admission reminded Hay Lin of the third, and final, reason the air felt so heavy that morning: Irma had just dished up a big buzz kill. Yesterday, at the Heatherfield Museum, she'd encountered a whole new Metamoorian invader—a big, green lizard.

Hay Lin had always had faith in fairies. After all, she'd been raised on her grandmother's fantastic fables. She'd actually traveled to another dimension, for Pete's sake. But even Hay Lin found it hard to envision a talking lizard, hanging out between the paintings and the sculptures at the Heatherfield Museum. It was just too weird!

"Are you really sure?" she asked Irma.

"Believe me, Hay Lin," Irma said. The teasing glint that usually danced in Irma's wide, blue eyes was completely AWOL. "If this dude wasn't a Metamoorian, then he was doing a brilliant impression of one."

Taranee folded her arms over her chest. The humidity had flattened her beaded braids onto her shoulders. It seemed also to have dampened her mood. She was looking majorly freaked. Of course, that was not unusual for Taranee. She was the most skittish of all the Guardians.

"The newspapers and TV reporters don't seem to have taken our lizard friend too seriously," she said, with a quiet sigh of relief. "They talk about it as if it were a kind of mass hallucination!"

"Well, we know the truth," Will said with a definitive nod at Irma. "After all, the lizard knew you were a Guardian."

Will glanced around the circle. Hay Lin could almost see the wheels turning behind Will's brown eyes. Will might have been a reluctant leader, but that didn't stop her from considering every move very carefully.

"Listen," she asked the girls. "Do you have any plans for after school?"

"I should hit the books," Irma said, slumping against the breezeway railing. "I've totally fallen behind on my schoolwork in the past few weeks."

"Oh, really?"

That was Cornelia. Her smile contained a mocking glint. "Weren't you the one who could rig any test with your amazing mental powers,

Irma?" She finished her thought and smiled smugly.

"Hey," Irma said. "Who asked you anything?"

Here we go again, Hay Lin thought. It's the Cornelia-and-Irma show. Cornelia irritates Irma, and Irma annoys Cornelia, and so on and so forth. Sometimes, all that 'tude annoyed Hay Lin. But this morning, she found it almost comforting!

At least one thing in our crazy lives these days is consistent! she thought.

As if to illustrate Hay Lin's point, Irma turned her back on Cornelia with a dramatic flourish and spoke directly to Will. "So, what are you thinking, Will?"

"It shouldn't take too much time," Will said. "I just think we need to understand why one of those creatures was in the museum. But how do we figure it out?"

Hay Lin's face lit up.

"I know!" she cried. She swung her bulging purple backpack off her shoulders and began rifling through it. She pushed aside a few sparkly Magic Markers, a pair of blue goggles, and the almond cookies she'd grabbed from her parents' Chinese restaurant earlier. Finally, she found what she was looking for—the magical map that came alive every time the girls discovered a portal. Hay Lin had a feeling that Irma's museum trip might have brought out a new bright spot on the dusty old parchment.

"Let's take a look," she declared, pulling the scroll out of her backpack.

"The map of the portals," Taranee said. She glanced at the busy students milling about. The coast was clear, but she still looked edgy.

"Shouldn't you keep that in a safer place?" she asked Hay Lin.

"There's no safer place than my backpack," Hay Lin replied as she unfurled the map. "It's my lifeline. I've got it with me all the time."

Hay Lin dropped to her knees and flattened the map out on the breezeway's stone floor. Will crouched down next to her and peered at the detailed rendering of Heatherfield. Then she gasped.

"Wow," she said. "Look there!"

"Yup!" Cornelia said excitedly as she, too, bent over to peer at the map. "Looks like we've located another of our twelve portals! At the Heatherfield Museum!"

"And *what* is so interesting, young ladies?"

Hay Lin froze. So did her friends. There was no mistaking the bold, brassy voice that had just rung out behind them. It was Mrs. Knickerbocker. *Principal* Knickerbocker. Sheffield Institute's very own white-haired dictator. She knew all. She saw all. And she didn't like it when her students tried to keep things from her.

Hay Lin's breath quickened, coming in short, dry gasps as she rerolled the magic map. And she'd thought the air was thick before! She bent over her backpack, struggling to stash away the secret treasure. As she yanked at her bag's zipper, the other Guardians formed a protective wall in front of her.

Irma piped up, "Tell us, Mrs. Knickerbocker. What *is* so interesting?"

"Uh-huh," Hay Lin heard the principal say. "Stalling for time. I admire your effort, Miss Lair, even if it isn't very original. But what I'd *really* like is to see the object of your attention. After all, there should be no secrets between a principal and her students."

"Of course!" Taranee squeaked.

Meanwhile, Hay Lin was frantically muttering to herself under her breath.

"Of all the times for my backpack zipper to get stuck," she whispered desperately.

"Hay Lin!"

Mrs. Knickerbocker's bellowing jolted Hay Lin to her feet. She thrust the map behind her back and flashed the principal a wide—if tremulous—grin.

"Yes?" she replied in a shaky voice.

"What are you hiding behind your back?" Mrs. Knickerbocker demanded. Her jowly, wrinkly face contorted itself into a grotesque scowl. "And I warn you, an answer like 'Which back?' will not be accepted."

"It's n—n—nothing, ma'am," Hay Lin stuttered. "It's only a drawing!"

Mrs. Knickerbocker glared down at her and said, "And so? Let's have a look at it! I'm curious as to what kind of drawing would hold five girls' interest so intensely!"

A drawing! Hay Lin thought desperately. She squeezed her eyes shut for an instant, focusing every brain cell on the idea. She willed her magic to well up within her.

It was working! Hay Lin felt a familiar tingling in her fingertips; a quickening of her heartbeat; and a floaty feeling that suffused every limb and made the ends of her pigtails swirl around her elbows. She sensed a stream of silvery magic emanating from her hands, which were still clutching the scroll behind her back.

When the fluttery feeling ceased, Hay Lin took a big gulp and handed the map to Mrs. Knickerbocker.

"Er, um, here it is," she whispered.

She cringed and waited for the principal's reaction.

"But—but—" Mrs. Knickerbocker stammered. Her eyes widened.

Oh, no! Hay Lin thought as she panicked. She glanced guiltily at her friends. We're sunk!

"This is incredible," Mrs. Knickerbocker continued. "It's me! And a perfect likeness. How did you do it?"

The shocked woman flipped the parchment around and showed it to the girls. The map had disappeared! In its place was a quick, slick pencil drawing of Mrs. Knickerbocker! It *was* a perfect likeness, from her cotton candy–like bouffant to her severe suit.

"Yes, Hay Lin," Cornelia breathed, her

cheeks flushed. "How *did* you do it?"

"Oh, well," Hay Lin scoffed, casting her eyes downward. "It was nothing."

"I knew drawing was your passion," Mrs. Knickerbocker said. "But this is amazing! It's a small masterpiece. May I have it?"

"No!" screeched every last Guardian. Mrs. Knickerbocker was so startled she dropped the scroll. Hay Lin plucked it from the air and rolled it up quickly. Then she shot the principal a quick grin.

"You see, this is only, well, a draft!" she improvised. "You deserve a much more beautiful picture, Mrs. Knickerbocker!"

A blip of suspicion flashed in the principal's pale eyes. But when Hay Lin grinned at her even harder, she relented and smiled back.

"All right, Hay Lin," she said. "I'll look forward to seeing that next drawing. I'll even put it up in my office."

Having said that, Mrs. Knickerbocker bustled away, and the five girls sagged with relief.

"What a con artist!" Irma exclaimed, looking at Hay Lin. "She deserves a 'more beautiful picture,' huh?"

Hay Lin shook her head and unrolled the

"drawing." A sparkle of magic shimmered across Mrs. Knickerbocker's image, melting it away. A second later, the original map of Heatherfield and its Metamoorian portals was restored.

"You should be thanking me," Hay Lin responded, sticking her tongue out at Irma. "If she had discovered our magic map, we would have had a big problem on our hands."

"If she had discovered the map," Cornelia said, glaring at Hay Lin, "it would have been your fault! We have to take better care of our secrets."

Hay Lin rolled the map up again. She felt a stab of guilt in her chest—another thing that made it hard to breathe! Cornelia was always hurling accusations. This time, however, she was right. She'd endangered the Guardians' mission, not to mention her grandmother's final gift to her.

Hay Lin felt hot tears well up in her eyes at the thought of her tiny grandmother's sweet face and long, white hair. She also thought of her grandmother's power. Right before her grandmother had died, she'd told Hay Lin that she, too, had been a Guardian as a young girl.

It turned out saving the world ran in the family! And that was nothing to be taken lightly.

"I hear you," Hay Lin said to Cornelia quietly. She tucked the map—carefully—back into her backpack.

"So, are we all right?" Will asked as she placed a gentle hand on Hay Lin's shoulder. Hay Lin smiled at her wanly.

With my friends at my side—through both mistakes *and* triumphs—I guess I *am* all right, she thought. She nodded at Will.

"Ready for action," she declared.

"Good," Will said. Her eyes grew dark and filled with determination. "Because the Heatherfield Museum closes at six tonight."

FIVE

"The Heatherfield Museum closes at six tonight."

As Uriah said those words, his voice almost cracked. He was *that* excited.

Of course, that was the last thing he wanted his gang to know. Excitement equaled weakness. Excitement was *not* cool.

And Uriah was cool at all costs.

He was the king of the Outfielders at Sheffield Institute. The Outfielders were the kids on the fringe—and the kids most often in trouble.

Uriah leaned against the railing of the Sheffield Institute breezeway. He toyed with the stiff spikes he'd molded into his bright red hair with gel. The rain was making them sag. He watched scornfully as Infielders hurried to beat the morning bell, which was going to ring in about five minutes.

See, that's the problem with being an Infielder, Uriah thought. You've got to follow the rules.

He watched with disdain as pretty girls swung their hair over their shoulders while they hurried to their lockers. Then he gazed across the rainy courtyard to the soccer field. Buff guys were trotting off the muddy pitch like earnest and obedient sheepdogs.

Completely conventional—all of 'em. Uriah scoffed.

Of course, conventional, Uriah thought, equals popular. And at Sheffield Institute, the popular ones are Infielders. Well, *I'm* proud to be an Outfielder—a loner. I don't need nobody.

The fact that Uriah was virtually never alone, that he was constantly tailed by his motley crew of thugs—well, that didn't really mean much. *Uriah* didn't need those dudes hanging around him. They needed him! They needed his power. His leadership. His smarts.

Especially tonight.

"So," Uriah said, casually picking at a zit on

his chin. "If the museum closes at six, we arrive at six-thirty. Work for you?"

"Okay by me," said Laurent. His eyebrows waggled wildly. He was psyched, too.

"Uh-huh," Kurt agreed through a giant mouthful of his breakfast sandwich—a smelly mix of pastrami, sauerkraut, and pickle relish.

Uriah flashed a thin-lipped grin at the two dudes. Laurent's barrel-chested brawn and Kurt's roly-poly heft would come in handy if they ran into any nosy guards at the museum.

Not that I *need* them or nothing, Uriah thought with a sniff. I'm *still* a loner. They'll just come in handy, is all.

Ah, but what about Nigel? Uriah thought. His eyes swung downward. Just as he'd expected, Nigel was sitting on the floor, leaning unobtrusively against the breezeway banister. His thin, tanned face looked morose and his brown eyes seemed troubled. Nigel, thought Uriah, was one sniveling puppy dog of a gang member.

I oughtta cut him loose right now, Uriah thought in annoyance. Dude's completely lost his edge. Some girl—like his mother—must have gotten under his skin!

Uriah glared at Nigel.

"I *said*, does that work for you, Nigel?"

"Huh?" Nigel stammered, gazing up at Uriah. "Uh, yeah, sure. There's just one thing I don't get. Why are we going to the museum after closing time?"

"To have fun, dork," Uriah sputtered. "To have fun."

Did he have to spell everything out for these lame-os?

Uriah checked out Laurent's vacant, slack-jawed stare, Kurt's flabby belly and yellow teeth, and Nigel's baby-smooth skin and floppy brown hair. He sighed. Amateurs! He *did* have to spell his plan out. Which stank, because spelling was his worst subject.

"Listen," he began irritably. "Rumor's going around that there's a monster or a ghost or somethin' at the Heatherfield Museum."

Nigel had pulled himself to his feet and was beginning to plod down the breezeway to the main building, heading for his first-period class. Shrugging, Uriah fell into step beside him. Naturally, Laurent and Kurt followed.

"If the rumor's true," Uriah continued, "I want to see it."

"But that's just gossip," Nigel protested. "And we could get into big trouble!"

"So?" Uriah snapped. "Nothing ever *happens* in this dump of a city."

Just the thought of it ticked Uriah off. He stomped up the stone steps of the main school building with such force he could feel his skinny knees jangling. He needed some action. It wasn't right to keep growing guys cooped up in—ugh—school! It wasn't natural, when you thought about it.

"Y'know," Kurt said, taking another monstrous bite of his sandwich, "Uriah's right. This place's a sleeper."

"That's the problem," Uriah said. "I'm *bored*, man!"

Nigel shot Uriah an alarmed, wide-eyed stare. It was clear that he'd rather be safe—and bored—than seek adventure with his crew.

Uriah rolled his eyes. Lame! He tried to console himself by imagining what Nigel would look like tonight, when he ran into some creature from the black lagoon–type thing in the dark halls of the Heatherfield Museum. It would be better than a horror movie, *without* the price of admission.

Uriah almost jumped up and down at the thought. But just before his oversized high-tops left the floor, he squelched the impulse. Bouncing around in excitement? *Definitely* uncool.

So instead, Uriah just slung his arm around Nigel's shoulders. He leaned all his weight on the skinny kid, making him stumble and struggle. As Nigel winced with discomfort, Uriah grinned with satisfaction. Then he declared, "Tonight's gonna be different! Tonight is mine. It's gonna be Uriah's world!"

SIX

Cornelia looked at her watch, then huffed in frustration. She couldn't see the time. It was too dark, as she crouched in the shadows next to the Heatherfield Museum's front steps.

Luckily, Will had had the same impulse. And while Cornelia's watch was a fancy, gold one, Will's was chunky, with a glow-in-the-dark face. When she pressed a button on the watch's edge, a smiling frog on the face glowed green, and Will could read the time.

"It's six-fifteen," she murmured.

Cornelia gazed at the glowy little frog. Will's passion for frogs was just *one* of the things Cornelia didn't get about her new friend. Even when she had been little, Cornelia had never gone gaga over stuffed animals or stickers. After all, she'd been a serious skater since she was six. And when it came to fashion, Cornelia had always been more comfortable in a flowing skirt and sassy little shawl than Will's look— slouchy jeans, gummy bracelets, an array of hoodies, and slumped shoulders to match.

Cornelia sighed. She felt weary. She felt old—older, anyway, than her fellow Guardians. Did the others really understand how low they'd all sunk?

We're one step away from becoming total hoodlums! Cornelia thought, feeling a tiny flutter of panic in her chest. After all, we've been sneaking into places on a weekly basis. First it was Elyon's abandoned house, then our math teacher's hall closet. But tonight, it's the Heatherfield Museum, which is a much bigger deal. If we're caught, they'll throw us in jail! And I can't really see us saving the world if we're stuck behind bars!

Hopefully, Cornelia thought, gritting her teeth, our magic will make sure that that doesn't happen.

Once again, Will's thoughts seemed to echo Cornelia's own. Will clenched her right hand in a fist and glanced at her companions.

"Are we ready?" she asked them.

"The coast is clear, Will," Cornelia said, glancing around. "Nobody in sight."

Will flashed Cornelia a grateful smile—one that made Cornelia feel a twinge of guilt. She'd been chafing under Will's leadership ever since the girls had become Guardians. She'd questioned everything Will had said—or simply looked sullen and surly while Will spoke.

Lately, Cornelia had to admit, Will had been leading them with a bit more confidence. Cornelia couldn't help being comforted by that as Will got ready to transform the five ordinary girls into superhuman Guardians.

"Okay," Will whispered to the group. "Come closer to me."

Cornelia and company crowded in. When they'd formed a tight circle, Will closed her eyes and squeezed both hands at her sides. Cornelia watched as Will's face grew animated. It almost looked as if she were having a silent conversation with some heavenly force. Then, beams of glowing, bright-pink magic began to peek through her right fist. Will threw her head back, her back arching and legs tensing.

She gasped. Magic was surging through her!

As the magic crested, Will thrust out her fist and unclenched her fingers. Hovering above her palm was the Heart of Candracar. Within its asymmetrical silver clasp, the marble-sized glass orb pulsed with power.

"Hay Lin," Will cried. "Air!"

A silver teardrop of magic shot out of the Heart and soared over toward the smallest Guardian. She threw her arms above her head in a gesture of freedom as the teardrop whizzed around her, transforming her from girl to, well, supergirl!

"Irma," Will shouted next. "Water!"

This time the magic teardrop was blue.

Then Will sent a fiery orange one to Taranee.

Finally, she turned to Cornelia. Cornelia gulped at the air, like someone preparing to plunge into a cold lake.

"Cornelia," Will shouted. "Earth!"

The magic teardrop was green this time. Cornelia braced herself as the orb began to whirl around her, leaving trails of magic on her skin like a gossamer sheath.

Cornelia felt her eyes squeeze shut and her head move backward. Her transformation from girl to Guardian had begun.

Its first glimmer was a surge of heat in Cornelia's chest. Within seconds, the warmth morphed into jets of electric energy, shooting up her arms. Cornelia could actually feel her muscles lengthening and tightening.

She gasped.

After that, her mind shut down. She felt her body contract as the magic suffused her every cell. Her clothes began to swirl away. Cornelia felt her legs lengthen and her body change. Delicate, feathery wings unfurled from her back with a soft, crackling sound. She felt her blond hair—silkier and smoother and even longer than before—fall gracefully around her shoulders. And, at last, the pressure caused by the transformation eased. When Cornelia opened her eyes, she saw that her friends had also completed their miraculous mutations.

The five girls blinked at each other, admiring their funky, striped leggings, their fluttery wings, their kickin' skirts and midriff-baring tops. They also appraised—a bit shyly—the now grown-up bodies within those cool outfits.

They had become women. Wise, beautiful, magical, and, most of all, strong!

And they were ready for their new, not-so-favorite after-school activity—breaking and entering.

"Where should we go in?" Irma asked, gazing with dread at the imposing, cryptlike museum.

"Let's try the windows in the back," Will suggested. She began to lead the group away from the building's front steps.

"But what about the alarms?" Cornelia asked. "Did you think of that, Will?"

"Sure!" Will said. Even in the dim light, Cornelia couldn't miss the flush of pride upon her friend's newly angular cheeks. "If my power works with the appliances in my house, it should work with the ones here, too!"

Oh, right, Cornelia thought. I'd almost forgotten about Will's bizarro ability to chat with her refrigerator (which even had the stuffy, British accent of a proper butler). Her computer and printer talked to her, too—when they weren't arguing with each other. In fact, Will could communicate with all of her electronic gadgets, from her cell phone to her cranky, old television set.

It was all a little too Saturday-morning-cartoon for Cornelia. She hated *cute* and made no secret of it. But now, Cornelia realized, with another twinge of guilt, Will's dorky power might really come in handy! If, that is, the museum's surveillance cameras cared to listen to her.

We'll find out soon enough, Cornelia thought as the girls rounded a corner and approached the back of the museum. There's a camera right next to that window near the Dumpster.

With her friends clustered behind her, Will positioned herself below the window.

"Um, excuse me?" she squeaked. "I was wondering if . . ."

"You're here about the creatures, yes?"

The camera was speaking to Will! Its red light flickered and flashed with every syllable. It spoke in a brisk, New England accent.

"Er—yes!" Will replied.

"But you are not policemen!" the camera said skeptically.

"Not exactly," Will said, with a shrug. "But, we might be able to figure out who the creatures are."

"Well . . ."

Cornelia held her breath. Had Will convinced the camera? Cornelia herself would have been a little less sweet, a little more authoritative.

"Okay, go in," the camera said at last.

Cornelia sighed, with a mixture of relief and a bit of disappointment.

Will's approach wins the game *again*, she thought. Huh!

As the girls prepared to enter, the camera warned them: "Remember, no funny stuff!"

"So trusting!" Taranee muttered sarcastically.

"It's a security camera," Irma pointed out. "It's only doing its job!"

Meanwhile, Will and Cornelia were eyeing the window. It was about eight feet off the ground, and there wasn't exactly a ladder lying in front of it. Taranee and Irma joined hands to give Will a boost. Balancing on her friends' strong arms, Will tentatively raised the window. It wasn't locked! Jackpot!

As Will slipped inside the museum, Cornelia watched her turn to the camera one last time.

"Is it really okay?" she asked cautiously.

"Go on!" the camera said impatiently to the

girls. "I'll close my eye."

The camera's red light went dark. Then Will was swallowed up by blackness as she shimmied through the window. The other Guardians gazed up after her, collectively holding their breath.

Where *is* she? Cornelia thought after a long, long moment.

Finally, Will stuck her head back out through the window.

"I don't see any guards," she whispered. "C'mon in!"

The other girls helped each other up into the window, one by one. Hay Lin, who could fly, after all, darted in last.

The girls began creeping quietly down a dark, echoing corridor toward the art wing. After a few minutes, they reached a small, shadowy gallery.

"Here it is!" Irma whispered. "This is where it happened. Do you sense anything?"

Cornelia looked around. All she saw were looming oil paintings, walls painted a golden ocher, and spotlights giving off a dim, after-hours glow. Will was the first to respond.

"I don't think so." Will said, shrugging.

"But the portal must be in here some-where," Hay Lin protested. She drifted further into the gallery. "Let's all concentrate."

The girls fanned out through the room. Will inspected each corner, and Irma peered up at the ceiling. Cornelia wandered over to a partic-ularly large, medieval painting. Then she gasped.

"Oh, no!"

"What is it?" Taranee squeaked, running over and clutching at Cornelia's shoulders. The other girls gathered around the painting, too.

"Look at this painting!" Cornelia cried.

She pointed a slender finger at the enor-mous canvas. It was a broad view of a medieval village, populated by hordes of plump and cheerful townspeople, bustling around a town square. Normally, Cornelia would have passed by that sort of traditional oil painting with no more than a glance.

But this painting had one detail—right there in the middle—that transfixed Cornelia. And not with transcendence.

No, this painted scene made her freeze in terror!

SEVEN

Cornelia trembled as she pointed at the painting. Her gesture sent fear surging through Will like a sudden chill. When *Cornelia* let her guard down, things were *not* good!

Taranee squinted at a gold plaque next to the picture's ornate, gilt frame.

"It's called *The Never-Ending Spring*, by Elias Van Dahl," she pointed out.

Will glanced at the painting. It was a picture of an ancient, European village. In a square fronting a huge, Gothic cathedral, dozens of townspeople were depicted bustling about, dealing with street merchants, walking animals to market, juggling. They smiled and laughed. It was a sunny scene.

It's pretty nice! Will thought. Much

cheerier than those dour Gothic paintings they show us at school. But is this any time for an art appreciation moment? How do I gently tell Cornelia to get with the pro—

"Look at that person there in the painting," Cornelia blurted out, butting in to the middle of Will's thoughts. "Near that house."

Will and the others followed Cornelia's finger, which pointed to a cluster of people in the center of the painting. Beneath the eaves of a homey Tudor cottage stood a teenage girl. Her straw-colored hair hung in two long braids. Her blue eyes were pale and wan. And on her long, light blue tunic was a symbol—an assemblage of green-and-white half-circles and triangles.

"Elyon!" Hay Lin cried.

"Oh, man!" Irma gasped as she peered at the tiny girl on the canvas. "If that isn't her, it looks a *lot* like her."

"How—how'd she get into the painting?" Taranee shrieked.

"Actually," said a bone-chilling voice. "I'm behind you, girls!"

The girls spun around in alarm. Elyon hadn't lied. In an instant, she'd somehow leaped from her spot in the painting to the gallery floor. Now she stood before them—a defiant enemy.

"You!" Irma said accusingly.

"Hello," Elyon said. Will winced. The Elyon she'd briefly known in Heatherfield had now all but disappeared. This girl was heartless. Her voice was dry as dust and full of cruelty. Her eyes were heavy-lidded and cold. And boy, was she angry!

A sense of foreboding filled Will's body.

Elyon, she told herself, isn't here simply to talk to us. She means us harm! I can feel it!

Will grabbed Taranee's arm and gave it a squeeze. At the same time, she turned to glance at Hay Lin. She was just opening her mouth to call out a warning when Elyon beat her to the punch.

"This time," the soulless girl announced, with an evil grin, "I've come to say . . . good-bye!"

Elyon lifted her hands and a surge of icy white power hurtled from her palms. The magic grabbed the Guardians before they could even begin to react. In an instant, the five girls found themselves trapped in a giant, clear bubble.

Will banged on the wall of the bubble with angry fists, but she knew it was probably to no avail. When the Guardians had been imprisoned in Metamoor, they'd been tossed into bubbles just like this one. It was as thin and flexible as cellophane, but, at the same time, as cold and impenetrable as a diamond. The girls were caught!

Elyon wasn't the only witness to their humiliation. While she gazed at her captives with a tight little smile, another figure emerged from a corner of the art gallery. He was clapping his hands, an amused smirk on his face.

"Good strike, Elyon," the man said. His face was pale and chiseled. A silky curtain of blond hair swung around his shoulders.

At the man's praise, Elyon's smile grew tighter.

"I'm becoming quite good, aren't I?" she said as she continued to stare the Guardians down. Then she spoke to the girls.

"As you can see," she pointed out, "I also have magical powers. And whether you like it or not, I'm stronger than all of you!"

Irma glared at Elyon. But when she turned to Will, her face was pale and filled with fear.

"That man," she said. "He's—"

"Cedric," Elyon confirmed. "My date from the bookshop."

Will cringed. Cedric! He was the one who'd lured Elyon away! He'd invited her to meet him for a date at the school gym. Boy-crazy Elyon had been so nervous, she'd begged Irma, Hay Lin, and Will to meet them there as well. But when the three girls had arrived, there'd been no sign of Elyon and Cedric. Instead, the girls had met a giant, blue, rock-headed thug and a hideous snake-man, both of whom had tried to throw the newly anointed Guardians into a fiery pit!

I'll never forget that snake-man's horrible red eyes, Will thought. Not if I live to be a hundred years old.

"When we first saw Cedric at the Halloween dance," Elyon reminisced giddily, "he looked like this. But you've also seen him in a very different light."

With that, Cedric began to change! His pointy chin got pointier. His steely, blue eyes morphed into reptilian, red slits. His torso expanded until it became a hulking thorax. And his legs turned into a long, slithery, green tail.

Will gasped in horror. The very snake-man she'd just been reminiscing about had suddenly appeared before them! He was Cedric! Or rather, Cedric was he!

Will gazed at Elyon with new horror. How could she align herself with someone so evil, so cruel, so, so uncute!?

"Surprised?" Elyon said. "Oh, I was like you, at first. But then Cedric told me things. Many things. Incredible secrets that, tonight, I want to share with you."

"What's happened to you, Elyon?" Will cried. "You're not the same!"

"Look who's talking," Elyon answered, with a dry laugh. "Look in the mirror, Will. In case you haven't noticed, you've sprouted a pair of wings!"

Will suddenly realized that she could, indeed, see her reflection in the glassy wall of the floating prison. When she focused on it, she almost cried out. She still wasn't used to this magical version of herself—tall and lithe, with a new, angular face, and curvy figure. It was all too unreal!

Will shook her head.

This is no time for an identity crisis, she

scolded herself. This is about Elyon!

So Will pressed her face to the interior of the bubble. Her own reflection blurred, but Elyon's frosty face became more focused. Will stared at her former friend with brutal intensity.

"Listen to me, Elyon," she implored. "Open your eyes. Forget Cedric. This world—earth—is your home."

"You're wrong, Will," Elyon said coolly. "I belong to Metamoor."

Cedric slithered forward. The curled end of his hideous tail rose from the floor and caressed Elyon's cheek. Will recoiled in disgust, but Elyon closed her eyes and smiled as if Cedric were nothing but a kindly father, patting her on the head.

"Metamoor belongs to you, princess," Cedric hissed through his jagged, reptilian teeth. "You and your brother, Phobos."

"Phobos!" Will gasped.

That was the name of the man depicted in the green-and-white symbol on Elyon's tunic—the Seal of Phobos. Many of the objects, in fact, that had tripped up both them *and* the baddies who had stalked the Guardians were marked with that seal. Will had seen it on a book that had spewed choking, black sludge all over Cornelia's bedroom and on the uniforms of the soldiers of the army that had chased them all over Metamoor.

Now Cedric was saying that the man behind the Seal was Elyon's brother?!

Of all the bizarre revelations Will had weathered since becoming a Guardian, this one was the strangest!

EIGHT

Elyon glared at the bubble she had just created. In the aftermath, her fingertips tingled, her head buzzed, and her vision went blurry. Mustering enough magic to ensnare the five Guardians of the Veil had been draining.

And hiding her shakiness from her former friends was more energy-sapping still.

But it was also a necessity. Elyon had to hide any—every—sign of weakness from those traitorous girls. She was royal. She was above them. She had more magic alone than the five of them put together.

The Guardians' bubble prison was floating in the middle of the gallery. Taranee was clutching Will's shoulders in fear. Irma's and Hay Lin's hands were clasped. And Cornelia was squeezed in the middle of the group, glaring at Elyon with hurt in her eyes.

Of the five angry looks trained on Elyon, this was the only one that gave her a minor twinge. After all, once upon a time, Cornelia and Elyon had been the best of friends. They'd exchanged notes in every class, and eaten lunch together at their "special" table in the school cafeteria. Elyon had known the nooks and crannies of Cornelia's room as well as she'd known her own. The girls had confided to each other about all their crushes and dreams.

Elyon perked up a bit as memories of a former life began to seep into her thoughts. That life was dim now. She could barely fathom what it had been like to gossip her way through classes and after-school snacks; to giggle her way through dates and soccer practice; to draw happy doodles on all of her notebooks; and to sit on the beach, simply enjoying the sun on her pale skin and the sound of the crashing waves. All of those joys were absent from the weatherless world that made up Metamoor.

Suddenly, a reprimanding voice rang through Elyon's head, making her wince slightly in pain. She took a deep breath.

Remember, it was all a lie.

To whom the voice belonged, Elyon wasn't sure. Cedric? Phobos? Herself?

All that really mattered was that the voice spoke the truth. Reminiscing about life on earth was as pointless as eating cotton candy. After all, Elyon's life on earth had been just as substanceless as feathery, spun sugar.

"Those days," she muttered to herself grimly, "are over now. And I'm going to tell these silly girls why."

Elyon took a deep, calming breath. As she did, she felt her fingers cease their trembling. Her heavy-lidded eyes brightened a bit. Her strength was returning. She was ready to share her story.

"My parents," Elyon began, "died when I was still a baby. Phobos found a nurse for me. He trusted this creature with my life."

Elyon watched the Guardians exchange wary glances. After a moment, they returned their attention to Elyon.

Elyon took another deep breath and continued. She made her voice flat and soulless. Emotion would sully her message. Emotion was her enemy.

"My nurse betrayed my brother's trust," Elyon said matter of factly. "She agreed to kidnap me with a couple of officials. They took me far, far away. They used the Seal of Phobos to open a portal in the Veil. And that is how I arrived here on earth."

"The two officials told everyone they were my parents," Elyon said. Images of the liars she'd called Mom and Dad flashed through her mind. She saw Mom's sweet, pointy-chinned face and coppery hair. She caught a glimpse of Dad's soft brown eyes and easy smile.

No!

Elyon forced those people—those traitors— out of her thoughts. They were not her parents at all. They never had been. Ever. And neither was the other one.

"My nurse," Elyon continued. "Well, you already know her. She changed herself into a woman with blond hair and big glasses. She bought herself a bunch of cardigan sweaters, and she found a job as a math teacher."

"Mrs. Rudolph?" Will asked.

Elyon nodded. She knew the Guardians had already discovered Mrs. Rudolph's other identity. When they'd accidentally seen their teacher in her Metamoorian form—big floppy ears, reptilian skin, and all—they'd freaked. In fact, they'd chased Mrs. Rudolph through a portal back to Metamoor. Now she was living in hiding, somewhere in Elyon's new world. But she'd still managed to help the Guardians when they'd been in need. The thought of it made a ball of fury well up inside of Elyon. She clenched her fists as she answered Will.

"Yes, Mrs. Rudolph," she said. "Under her watch, and those of my 'adopted parents,' I've grown up among you. Among deception and lies! I loved and respected a pair of traitors who tore me away from my *real* family."

"What—what are you saying, Elyon?" Cornelia whispered.

"The truth!" Elyon barked. She glanced fondly up at Cedric's snaky face. She barely even noticed anymore when he morphed from his handsome blond self into this leering, green, scaly one. In both guises, Cedric was her friend. Her mentor. And the source of her great gift—her power.

"Cedric opened my eyes," Elyon said to the Guardians. "Do you remember that afternoon after the Halloween party when Cedric invited me to his bookshop? I thought he was trying to get to know me better. But he already knew everything about me."

Elyon still remembered the rush of trepidation and excitement she'd felt when she had entered Cedric's store that day. Moments later—among stacks of dusty old books and streams of late-afternoon sunlight—Cedric had told her everything. He'd called her princess! Because that's what she was—the heir to Metamoor's throne.

"Suddenly, everything that had been hidden from me was brought to light," Elyon told her prisoners. "I finally knew who I was. And I also knew who *you* were. The Guardians of the Veil. The enemies of Metamoor!"

"Enemies!" Will burst out, pressing her hands to the wall of the bubble. "I don't know what 'truth' Cedric told you, but we have a different version. Elyon—"

"Shut up!" Elyon screamed. She ran up to the bubble and banged on its rock-hard surface with her fists. She felt a stab of pain travel up her skinny arms with every strike, but she couldn't contain her rage. First, her friends betrayed her. *Now* they tried to deceive her? To play with her head and make her question her beliefs? How *dare* they!

"Because of the Veil that you protect," Elyon gasped, "the people of Metamoor are bound to live inside a cage. They have no way out."

Elyon felt tears well up in her eyes. Oh, no! Tears were a sign of weakness. For an instant, Elyon tried to fight them. A moment later, she gave up. She was beyond caring about preserving her chilly demeanor. It was too late for that.

"Because of the Veil you protect," Elyon continued, her voice going shrill, "my brother, Phobos, has been looking for me for *years* without being able to find me. Because of the Veil you protect, my life was not my own! And that is why I hate you, Guardians."

Irma stepped to the front of the bubble and gazed pleadingly at Elyon.

"We were friends once," she whispered.

"That's right, Irma," Elyon said, backing away from the bubble. "But I don't know you anymore. Look at yourselves. You've grown up. You've become so beautiful. You've changed!"

"You've changed, too!" Hay Lin cried.

Elyon's rage ebbed away. Her anger was replaced by a dull, pounding pain deep in her gut. Hay Lin was right. She took a deep breath.

"I have changed," Elyon said proudly. Cedric's tail coiled around her protectively as she spoke. "After I stopped the impostors who told me they were my parents, and after I passed though the Veil and found my real home in Metamoor, I discovered the real me."

"And you discovered hidden powers," Cedric prompted in his hissing, slithery voice.

"Yes," Elyon agreed.

Elyon raised her hands. She looked at them contemplatively as she prepared herself for what she was about to do. Her body began to hum with the tremendous power the task would require. Every muscle began to tighten painfully. Her fingertips spat white-hot sparks, and the pain in her gut mounted.

But Elyon's mind was numb.

Which only made her job easier.

Kzaaaaammmm!

"Feel that?" Elyon shouted as she hurled a concentrated shower of magic at the Guardians' bubble. The magic formed a crackling band that stretched between Elyon and the cell. It began to rattle. "It's called 'absolute power'!" Elyon shook with power.

"*Aaaaiggh!*" Taranee screamed inside the bubble. She looked to Will for guidance. "What's happening?"

Ha! Elyon thought. Even the Keeper of the Heart can't worm her way out of this one.

"I don't know," Will shouted. "But we've got to get out of this prison. Come on—let's try together to break out of here!"

Elyon began to laugh as she watched the girls pound together on the magic bubble.

"Nuh-uh, girls," she taunted. "It's no use! You've lost! And soon you'll understand all of Metamoor's pain. Soon you'll understand what it means to live as prisoners, far from every-thing . . . *forever!*"

Elyon gave the band of magic a final thrust. Then she threw her hands down, breaking the connection between herself and the bubble. The prison evaporated into thin air.

But the Guardians weren't freed. Instead, they began to hurtle into oblivion—a vacuum with no dimensions, no time, no space! An exile like no other!

The girls became wispy, ephemeral, and increasingly tiny. In a few moments, Elyon could barely see them anymore. But she could hear their final screams before a great white light swallowed them up.

The sound made her smile tightly.

And then, the Guardians were gone. Nothing remained of five human lives but a wisp of steam, a remnant of magic.

"Excellent, Elyon!" Cedric cried, clapping his hands together again. The sound echoed on the gallery's cold walls. "Really excellent."

Elyon tried to smile, but she found she couldn't. She was too drained to feel triumph.

Revenge must be like cotton candy, too, she mused dully. Its sweetness melts away in an instant.

"Prince Phobos will be satisfied," Cedric continued. His exaltations jangled through Elyon's head like the incessant tolling of a bell. "Candracar's five little meddlers are not a problem anymore. This time, nothing will be able to save them!"

NINE

Kurt plodded up the stone walkway to the Heatherfield Museum. He was trailing behind Uriah, focusing on the gang leader's floppy red sneakers. Every time Uriah lifted his foot, Kurt tried to put his own tattered, red high-top in the exact same spot.

This was a little game Kurt liked to play. He imagined he was a soldier, tracking an enemy through the snow. He'd come up with it because he *always* seemed to be trailing Uriah. He followed him from the 'hood to school, from school to detention, and from detention to whatever scheme his redheaded mentor had cooked up next.

This scheme is the coolest one yet, Kurt thought with a guttural giggle. We're breaking into the museum to battle a monster. Like Knight Schneider in *Goth Slam II*! Yeah! *Byrrr! Byrrr! Byrrr!* I got you, dragon! *Yah-ha!*

"Kurt!" Uriah hissed. He stopped so suddenly that Kurt plowed right into his bony back. Well, his stomach did, anyway. Kurt's stomach arrived everywhere about a half second before the rest of him.

Uriah glared over his shoulder at Kurt.

"Shaddup!" he hissed. "You want us caught before we even get in there? Doof!"

"I didn't say nothin'," Kurt protested.

"You're dead, dragon," Laurent teased. He shoved at Kurt with his meaty fist.

"Oh, uh, did I say that out loud?" Kurt said. He felt his eyes bugging out in confusion. "Whoops."

"Whatever," Uriah said. He rolled his eyes. "Just can it once we're in the museum. You don't want to be the weak link in the gang, do ya?"

"Hey, too late," Laurent guffawed.

"Guys," Nigel said nervously. Kurt glanced back at him. He was trailing reluctantly behind all of them. "Would you . . . would you just please keep it down? C'mon!"

Kurt clamped his fleshy lips together as the

gang sauntered around the museum. It wasn't hard. He just willed himself to stop thinking about video game dragons. Instead, he thought about . . . lunch! Today he'd made himself a few roast-beef sandwiches. With Snack Doodles thrown in for crunch and Tasti-whip, straight from the can, for dessert. Yummmmm . . .

"Lookit!" Laurent said, interrupting Kurt's daydream. "They even left the window open."

Kurt blinked. Sure enough, Laurent was pointing up at a wide-open window.

"Aw," Kurt groused. "And they say they don't *want* people to steal from museums. They shouldn't be so careless."

"Don't complain!" Uriah said with a devilish grin. "Follow me."

Uriah catapulted his skinny self up to the window ledge. He slipped through the open window as slickly as a snake.

"Uh-oh," Kurt whispered. The window was at least eight feet off the ground. Kurt barely cleared five. He gave Nigel and Laurent pleading glances.

They looked pointedly at his jiggling gut.

They gazed up at the window.

After a few complaining sighs, they finally

joined hands and kneeled in front of Kurt. Flashing them a grateful grin, Kurt stepped into the boost and scrambled up the museum wall. He flopped his upper body through the open window.

"Dude!" Nigel grunted from his spot on the ground. "Time to cut down on the snacks!"

Kurt flailed his short legs around in an effort to squirm the rest of himself through the window. Finally he made it, landing on the marble floor with a fleshy splat.

I'm in, he thought with relief.

While Laurent and Nigel hoisted themselves through the window after him, Kurt pulled a flashlight out of the back pocket of his baggy jeans. He clicked it on and followed Uriah into the main corridor of the museum. It was a long aisle, lined with a bunch of medieval artifacts.

Kurt's flashlight beam swept across coats of arms, moldy old tapestries, and tarnished suits of armor.

Museums, he thought dully. Educational. *Soooo* borrrrring. *Yawwwwn.*

He plodded along. But as his flashlight glimmered off another suit of armor, a realization suddenly wormed its way into his head.

Hey, wait a minute, he thought. Those are *knights'* clothes. Like Knight Schneider. Yeah!

Before he knew it, Kurt was back in *Goth Slam II*. He could almost hear the metallic clang of a sword landing on a steel breastplate. Yeah! *Byrrr! Byrrr!*

"Kurt!" Laurent hissed, jolting Kurt out of his video game fantasy. "Turn that flashlight off, man!"

Kurt stuck his lower lip out, but he obeyed Laurent's orders. As the flashlight went black, Kurt blinked hard. He was seeing spots—and little else.

"We should be as quiet as cats," Uriah announced to the guys as they approached the end of the aisle. A door at the corridor's end led to the museum's art wing. That was where the monster was rumored to be lurking.

"Yeah," Uriah continued with a cackle. "We'll pretend we're pumas."

Pumas! Kurt perked up. Pumas were even cooler than knights!

"Yeah, yeah," Kurt giggled. "Quiet, like pumas!"

Kllaaaannnnggg! Crash. Rattle-rattle-rattle.

"Owwwww," Kurt groaned. He shook his head and swiped a hank of mud-brown hair out of his eyes. When he looked around, his eyes widened.

Now he really *was* starring in his very own episode of *Goth Slam II*! His pudgy fingers were closed around the hilt of a medieval sword and he was surrounded by—knight parts! There was an arm in his lap, a foot a few feet away, even a knight's head bobbling around him like a runaway hubcap!

Did I black out while I was waging battle? Kurt wondered. *Am I a war hero?*

Uh, that would be a big no.

But Kurt *was* a klutz who'd crashed right into a suit of armor. That fact was confirmed by Uriah's wrathful, spotty face, swooping in close to snarl at him.

"What are you doing?" he hissed.

"Not my fault," Kurt grunted. He used the sword to push himself to his feet. "You made me turn off my flashlight. I can't see anything!"

Nigel trotted over. *His* face was paler than the moonlight shining through the museum windows.

"If there are security guards around, they *definitely* heard that noise," he gasped. "Let's get outta here!"

"If you want to leave, do it," Uriah said with a threatening sneer on his face. "But you'll hafta get past me!"

Uriah turned to face his crew head-on. As he lectured them, he started backing up. He was moving toward the door that led to the art galleries—and blocking Nigel's path. With each step away from his crew, he became fuzzier, melting into the shadows of the dark corridor.

"We've come here to catch a monster," Uriah declared from the dark. "And we ain't leaving until we see at least one!"

Bump!

"Oof!" Uriah grunted. He'd knocked into something. Kurt cringed, waiting for a crash of armor. Or the clattery tumble of a tapestry.

Instead, he heard a voice. It was a growly voice—both sinister and smirking. And it came from very, very high above the gang.

"Are you looking for something, boys?" the voice said.

Suddenly, a man—make that a creature!—stepped into the gallery. He was about a dozen feet tall, with an angry red mask over his eyes. He had green, reptilian skin, a long shock of dusty blond hair, and a snaky tail that slithered around the gallery like a sensor.

Next to the terrifying figure was another monster. This one was bright blue! He was half the snake-man's height, but twice his girth. The lumpish horns on his head resembled rocks. His jagged teeth were bared as he growled at the boys.

Uriah squealed as the snake-man gave him a shove. He fell sprawling on the floor. Laurent shrieked loudly and stumbled backward. Nigel stood frozen beside Kurt, his face even whiter than before.

The loudest scream of all didn't come from Laurent, Kurt, or even Nigel.

"AAAGHHH!" Uriah cried, with his face frozen in fear.

But Kurt didn't feel terrified. Not exactly. He didn't feel brave, either. What he felt like was a warrior!

Kurt planted his fleshy feet on the marble floor. He tightened his grip around the sword that was, miraculously, still clutched in his hand. He was ready to fight!

TEN

Cornelia was sure she was the first of her friends to recognize what Elyon had just done to them.

Elyon and Cornelia had been best friends once. If anyone understood how Elyon's mind worked, it was Cornelia. And here's what Cornelia knew: before Elyon had defected to Metamoor, she had longed for escape of a different kind. She had never liked the messiness of real life—unrequited crushes, nasty school lunches, annoying parents, math homework.

Whenever these things had really freaked her out, Elyon had retreated into art, drawing and painting for hours. Art was where Elyon had felt most at home.

So, now, she's made a work of art *our*

home, Cornelia thought. She's sent us into that painting. We've replaced her there!

Grimly, Cornelia surveyed the scene in which the Guardians had just landed.

They were standing by a well made of rough-hewn stone. The street beneath their feet was made of roughly packed dirt. Bustling all around them were plump townspeople. The women wore long, homespun skirts, bonnets, and tight bodices bound by leather laces. The men wore suede breeches and belted tunics.

Everyone was busy carrying bulging baskets of bread, vegetables, and meats. Or juggling cannonballs. Or carting banners to a stage in the town square. The banners—fluttering in a sweet-smelling breeze—were printed with suns, flowers, blooming trees, dancing figures, and other symbols of spring.

The townspeople laughed and gossiped. They looked robust and happy. And thus—to Cornelia, at least—they were unspeakably annoying.

These people, she thought incredulously, aren't just stuck in a time warp. They're mired in permanent good moods! And why shouldn't they be? *They* don't have to save the world with their brand-new magical powers. *They* haven't been banished from their homes by a girl with a serious chip on her shoulder. No, they're simply the stars of *The Never-Ending Spring*. We're part of an invention by What's-his-name Van Dahl!

Hey, wait a minute, Cornelia realized suddenly. Magical powers! I almost forgot! I'm Earth Girl. And what are we standing upon except earth?

Cornelia glanced down at her purple boots. They were smudged with some sort of yellow-brown pigment.

Well, she corrected herself, we're standing on paint that's made to look like earth. Let's hope that's close enough for me to get us out of here! I'll just create a fissure in the earth, and that should rip open the painting's canvas! Sure, it'll mean sacrificing a work of art, but at least we'll be free!

Cornelia gave her friends a sidelong glance. She supposed she should bounce her escape plan off Will before she began to summon up her magic.

But it was Cornelia's idea! If she was successful, not only would the girls be free of this ridiculous painting, but they'd have Cornelia to thank for it! It might have been petty, but *she* wanted to be the hero once in a blue moon. It was weird always being in Will's shadow.

So—after shooting the jolly townspeople a disdainful, good-bye glance—Cornelia closed her eyes. She sent all her magical energy down to her toes. Behind her closed eyelids, she saw waves of green. Then she felt her entire body begin to thrum with power.

When her magic hit its peak, Cornelia willed herself and her friends out of the painting. In fact, she envisioned them outside of the museum entirely. She'd send them to a grassy refuge or the cradle of a craggy tree.

She'd bring them home.

At last, Cornelia felt her magic melt away. The deed was done. Opening her eyes, she blinked away a few green spots and looked around triumphantly. She couldn't wait to see where the Guardians had landed. They were—

Still in the painting!

Cornelia's mouth dropped open. She and her friend hadn't budged an inch!

But that means, Cornelia wailed inwardly, my magic is useless here! I guess there are *lots* of things I don't get about Elyon. Like all the tricks she has up her evil sleeve!

Cornelia glanced at her girlfriends' frightened faces. Then she took in all the chortling townspeople milling around them.

Fabulous, she thought irritably. Only minutes ago, we were the five most powerful beings on earth. We had the ability to change the elements, simply by wanting to. But, oh, how quickly things change. Now, we have *no* abilities. We're mere prisoners in a painting!

"Guys," Irma said in a tremulous voice. "I think we have a problem!"

"Where are we?" Hay Lin cried. "What is this place?"

"Don't you get it?" Cornelia yelled. "We're in the painting. Elyon sent us here!"

Taranee gasped. She gaped at a nearby juggler. A couple of other guys were jostling past them with tent poles and canvas. They seemed to be setting up for some sort of outdoor play.

"Who are all these people?" she wondered.

Before the Guardians had a chance to ponder the question, one of the people in the crowd tripped and crashed right into Taranee! The man, who had a brushy mustache and a goofy fez atop his head, sank his elbow into her gut.

"Hey!" Taranee squealed. A fiery spark of anger clouded her face as she regarded the clumsy man. "Why don't you look where you're going?"

"And you!" the man responded. His jovial grin faded as he took in Taranee's striped leggings, bare belly, and sleek tendrils of hair.

Suddenly Cornelia got a sinking feeling in her stomach. Taranee looked like a *thoroughly* modern teenager. All the Guardians did. They really didn't fit into this antique scene.

"Where did you come from?" the man demanded.

His booming voice attracted the attention of the juggler. Not to mention a couple in expensive-looking, velvet robes.

"Look at them!" the juggler cried.

"Who are they?" cried the nobleman's wife.

"They must not be from our country," said another townsperson emphatically.

Cornelia clenched her hands in tight fists.

Here we go, she thought.

Another townie sidled up to the Guardians with an excited grin on her face.

"Are you wanderers?" she asked the girls.

"Where is your caravan?"

Yet another woman with a brown-wool shawl draped over her hair grabbed one of Will's wings and gaped at it.

"Maybe they're artists," she gasped. "Look at how they're dressed!"

"We dress circles around you, frumpy!" Irma yelled. "You can count on it!"

Cornelia rolled her eyes.

It didn't take Irma long to lose her cool, she thought. But what else was new?

Will tried to smooth things over.

"Irma," she whispered, grabbing her friend's elbow. "Let's beat it."

Quickly, the Guardians ducked into the crowd. Dodging their way around a peddler's pushcart and a snuffling mule, they lost the townspeople who'd been scrutinizing them. Now they were in a *new* crowd of people. It seemed that every inhabitant of the painting was thronging the streets!

Looking around her uncomfortably, Will whispered, "We need to get back to our old selves. We attract too much attention dressed like this."

"Okay," Hay Lin said, agreeing quickly with

Will. "Let's change, then."

Before Cornelia could discourage her, Hay Lin thrust her hands to her sides and closed her eyes. Her face scrunched with concentration. But no silvery swirls of magic emanated from her fingertips. When Hay Lin opened her eyes a moment later, she was still a glam superbabe. She gaped down at herself.

"B—but," she gasped.

"Nothing happened!" Will said, confused. "Why didn't we change?"

"Our powers don't work anymore," Cornelia announced sullenly. She'd just begun getting *used* to being magical. And now her powers were being snatched away? Could this whole Guardian gig be any *more* unfair?

"Powers?" asked a bewildered voice behind the Guardians. Cornelia covered her mouth and spun around to see a new group of townspeople giving the girls the fish-eye.

"What are they talking about?" a man in a pointy beard wondered aloud.

"They must be illusionists," said a round-cheeked woman. But she looked skeptical.

That was when three soldiers in leather armor, steel helmets, and tall, suede boots broke through the crowd. Resting his hand on the hilt of his sword, the head knight declared, "Or they might be something worse. Witches!"

"Uh . . . guys?" Will whispered to the other Guardians, backing up a step or two. "These people are afraid of us!"

"I'm more afraid of them," Hay Lin hissed back. She pointed at the soldiers' heavy swords. "They'll slice us into sushi!"

"If they manage to catch us!" Irma cried. She suddenly jumped out of the girls' cluster and ran to the edge of the street, where several merchants had set up their wares. She grabbed the edge of a fruitmonger's wooden table and gave it a mighty heave. Baskets of apples, pears, and melons went flying at the soldiers!

"It's an assault!" the head soldier cried. "Stop!"

And that's our cue to run! Cornelia thought. The girls turned on their heels and dashed into the crowd. But it was hard to really make a break for it with all those people milling around. Cornelia bumped into a doughy woman with a shopping basket on her arm. Irma tripped on the hem of another woman's long cloak. Taranee did a mad sidestepping-maneuver as she tried to dodge around a fortune-teller's table. She finally made it, but not without knocking the mystic's crystal ball to the ground.

"If we don't get out of this crowd, we're sunk," Cornelia announced, the sound of shattering glass ringing in her ears. "They'll catch up to us in a flash."

In fact, Cornelia could already hear the soldiers' gruff voices, wafting over the heads of the townspeople.

"Out of our way now!" one of the soldiers shouted gruffly.

"Stop the witches!" another commanded.

"But where do we go?" Hay Lin cried, spinning in a desperate circle.

Will bit her lip.

Where *do* we go? Cornelia thought. She felt a bubble of panic begin to rise in her chest. We're blocked in!

"I know!" Will suddenly gasped. She squinted at the sun mischievously. "We go up!"

Will pointed at the thatched roof of a nearby cottage. Of course! Up was their way out.

Cornelia pushed her long, flowing skirt out of the way and clambered onto a barrel. From there, she hoisted herself onto a narrow wall. Then, grabbing handfuls of the tightly packed straw, she pulled herself, hand over hand, up to the peak of the roof.

Her friends quickly followed her. When they all arrived at the rooftop, they saw that there were other buildings nearby.

Taller buildings.

Giving each other determined glances, they began climbing again. They tiptoed along the narrow ridgepole atop one roof, then climbed up the stone steps up to a stone turret. At the sound of the soldiers' angry voices, they sped up.

"Wherever we go," Cornelia complained, as she hopped from the turret onto another thatched roof, "someone is after us! In Metamoor it was the same thing!"

"I always dreamed of having people run after me—to get an autograph," Hay Lin sighed wistfully.

"Yeah, but these guys are running after us to disintegrate us," Taranee complained. She struggled to find her footing on the straw rooftop. "That's another thing entirely."

"There they are!" called a voice directly below them. It was the soldiers. They'd been following them through the streets. Now they were gazing up at them fiercely, their swords drawn.

"We're too visible up here!" Will cried, scrambling backward on the thatched roof. "Let's go *dow-WWWN!*"

As she spoke, Will's leg suddenly plunged through the straw! The rest of her body quickly followed.

"*Ooofff!*" Will shrieked as she hit the floor below.

"Will!" the rest of the Guardians cried. But they didn't have very much time to worry about their fallen comrade. They were slipping and sliding toward the hole themselves!

"We're *all* going down!" Irma yelled, scrabbling madly at the straw. It did no good, of course. Soon, all five girls had tumbled into the cottage.

"Ow!" Cornelia screamed as she landed on the dirt floor with a thud.

A housewife sat kneading bread nearby responded with a tremendous screech. That was followed by the slap of the cottage door as it flew open. Two of the helmeted soldiers crowded through the doorway. Their swords flashed in front of them as they glowered at the Guardians.

"You're trapped, girls," the head soldier announced.

"Oh?" Will said. Cornelia watched Will's large, brown eyes flicker to her right. Subtly, Cornelia glanced over, too. The Guardians were standing right next to the cottage's *back* door! And, in the one bit of luck they'd encountered since arriving in this inhospitable painting, the door was standing open.

"That's what everybody says to us," Will said to the soldiers impudently. "But anyone who knows us knows that we don't take 'trapped' for an answer!"

Cornelia dashed for the door, with her friends right behind her! Cornelia bounded down a couple of stone steps and scanned the cottage's yard quickly.

"This way!" she shouted, veering left. She glanced over her shoulder to urge her friends along. "Quick!"

Unfortunately, while Cornelia was peeking behind her, the *third* soldier was stepping right in front of her! Cornelia ran into his armored chest with a painful *thwack*! The goon's muscly arms closed around her like a vise.

"And you!" he demanded with an evil grin. "Where do you think you're going?"

"No!" Cornelia grunted, struggling within the soldier's grip. But without her magic strength, she was no match for the big brute.

I promise, Cornelia thought bitterly, *never* to complain about being magical again. If I had my powers right now, I'd wrap this guy in vines as thick as boa constrictors. I'd plant birds' nests in each of his ears. I'd turn his eyebrows into moss!

But in reality, all Cornelia could do was shoot her captor evil looks. He responded with a cocky grin as the other soldiers thundered out of the cottage.

"I've caught them, Captain," Cornelia's brute said, cruelly tightening his grip on her. Now the Guardians really were trapped.

But they weren't speechless.

"Leave me alone, you big, ole monkey!" Cornelia spat at her soldier. She twisted so violently in his grip she actually managed to turn her back on him completely.

That's when the soldier got a good glimpse of Cornelia's wings. His beady, brown eyes widened in shock. And then, in fear.

Aha, Cornelia thought. I'm not magic at the moment. But I still *look* it.

Mischievously, she flexed the muscles in her back, making her feathers flutter and twitch.

"What, what are these beings?" her captor asked. "Those wings! They're real!"

"Incredible," said one of the other knights. He stumbled forward to finger Cornelia's wings gingerly. She tried to shake him off. Her feathers were as soft as satin and as iridescent as a dragonfly's wing. They were her favorite part of her magical self, and she *didn't* want to share them. When the head soldier stepped forward with a curious look of his own, Cornelia gave him a swift kick in the shin. It worked. He stayed away from her wings.

But he *did* get angry. Very angry.

"Take them to the palace dungeon!" he ordered his underlings. "I'm going to inform Camerlengo immediately—"

"Don't be in such a big hurry, Captain Schliege," said a voice at the edge of the garden. Cornelia and her friends stared and froze in surprise.

More importantly, the soldiers froze as well! Everyone turned to watch a brown-haired fellow stride into the yard.

"You!" the leader hissed, staring at the man.

Cornelia wondered who the man could be. He certainly didn't *look* powerful enough to cow three armed knights. He had shaggy, brown hair that fell over his eyes and a thin, pale face. He was extremely slight. His chocolate-brown eyes were large and sad, but his mouth—behind a well-trimmed goatee—was tight-lipped and determined.

"The palace dungeon is not the right place for these kind girls," the man declared.

"Hear that, ya big monkey?" Irma cried. She ran over to Cornelia's captor and grabbed his arm with both hands, wrenching Cornelia from his grip. "Get your paws off of us, and get outta here. Immediately!"

The soldier obliged and unhanded Cornelia. But then he grabbed Irma! With her wrist held firmly in his meaty fist, he gazed pleadingly at the brown-haired mystery man.

"Can I take *her* away, at least?" he begged. "*She's* not very kind."

Cornelia stifled a snort of laughter.

"No," the man responded. "Inform Camerlengo that these girls are now my guests!"

"But," the soldier began to wheedle, "Mr. Van Dahl . . ."

The man shot the soldier a meaningful glare. That was enough to squelch the knight's protest completely. His shoulders slumped and he motioned brusquely to his men. Finally, all three of them stomped out of the yard.

When they'd disappeared, the Guardians encircled their savior. His glare disappeared. Now he merely looked weary. He gathered his flowing, orange cloak more closely around himself, as if he'd caught a sudden chill. The girls gazed at him in quizzical silence, until, of course, Irma spoke up.

"Thanks for your help, mister!" she chirped.

"Oh, no," the man protested, waving a hand humbly. "Please, just call me Elias."

"It didn't take much for you to chase off those soldiers," Irma said with a wide-eyed look. "You must be important, Elias!"

That's it, Irma, Cornelia thought. Don't mince words or anything. Just pry into the guy's business an instant after we've met him!

But Elias didn't seem to mind. He smiled

sheepishly and said, "After all these years, I still haven't figured out if they are afraid of me or respect me. Certainly, they owe me a lot."

Cornelia frowned in confusion as she watched Elias gaze wistfully up at the sunny sky. Then he nudged at the painted dirt with the toe of his boot. Finally, he sighed and looked at the girls with a rueful smile.

"You see," he said wearily, "this sky, this town, these people, even—it's I who created them."

ELEVEN

Nigel wondered when he had last taken a breath.

It was definitely many minutes ago, he decided woozily. In fact, I must have passed out from lack of oxygen. Now I'm dreaming!

That was the only way to explain what he was seeing—a towering, red-eyed snake with long, white hair and a semihuman face!

And, it seemed, the snake-man could also speak, in English! When he and his walruslike blue henchman had lunged toward the gang a moment ago, he'd sounded none too happy to find the guys there.

That makes two of us, Nigel thought.

But Nigel didn't just want to escape the terrifying monsters. He also wanted to ditch the dudes at his side—his so-called friends.

Nigel glanced at Uriah and Laurent, both of whom were shrieking crazily.

Those tough guys would feed me to the monsters with a cherry on top if it would get them out of here in one piece, Nigel thought. Kurt, too.

Kurt. He was the only member of the crew more hapless than Nigel. Speaking of, where was he?

Nigel scanned the dark gallery for the gang's tubbiest member. When he spotted him, he gasped.

Okay, he thought, his eyes bugging out in shock. Now I *know* I'm dreaming. *Kurt* is our savior?

But it was true. Kurt had stepped out in front of the other guys. He was wielding a giant sword. The thing was so heavy he could barely lift it over his head. But if he knew how hopeless his heroics were, his face didn't show it. In fact, Kurt's doughy cheeks were flushed with excitement. Under his breath, he was whispering, "*Byrrr! Byrrr!* Take that, dragon!"

Great, Nigel thought. Now we've got two

cowards and a delusional maniac. And me? Well, I'm the idiot, thank you very much.

With a heavy sigh, Nigel realized he'd been living in this state of idiocy for a long time— ever since he'd started hanging with Uriah's gang.

He'd wandered thoughtlessly into his Outfielder status. But once there, he'd found it impossible to claw his way out. Now he was a permanent member of the crew. He was stuck.

Speaking of which, Nigel was still facing down the horrible monsters. And he was still struggling to take a breath! Just when he was sure his lips were turning blue, his lungs took over and clamored for air. Nigel gasped and sucked in a big gulp of oxygen. He took several deep, rattling breaths.

And then he blinked.

The snake-dude and the big, blue thug were still there. Which meant Nigel *hadn't* passed out and dreamed this up.

The monsters were real!

"Run away!" Uriah screamed, turning to dash back down the long museum corridor.

"*Tscha!*" Laurent cried, chasing after the gang leader.

But Kurt stood his ground! He even took a flat-footed step toward the big, blue guy, heaving the sword up in front of his face.

"Stand back!" he ordered the monster in a tremulous voice.

"Kurt!" Nigel cried. He stopped running, then glanced ahead at his fleeing buddies. He looked back at Kurt, quaking before the growling blue giant. What should he do? He couldn't just leave Kurt there to be squashed like a grape. But if he joined the fight, *he'd* be squashed, too!

Nigel shrugged and began running back toward his squat comrade. Before he could reach him, though, the monster leaned over and snarled in Kurt's face.

"Your defiance is very amusing, boy," he said. His voice sounded like gravel drenched in smelly tar. "But if you want to make a dent in me, you'll need something stronger than this toothpick!"

With another growl, the monster swatted at Kurt's sword. It sailed through the air like a dart, landing with a *thwack* in the middle of an oil painting—a very famous still life.

"Aaaagh!" Kurt cried. His eyes widened, as

if he, too, were just waking up from a dream. The monster laughed cruelly. Then he lunged at the pudgy kid.

Nigel's feet once again began to move, almost against his will. Before he had a chance to think, he'd grabbed Kurt's shirt collar and yanked him out of the monster's reach.

"Run, Kurt!" he cried, struggling to pull his portly friend down the museum corridor.

Nigel huffed in relief as Kurt finally began to follow him. Together, the boys made a run for it.

But they didn't stay together for long! While Nigel headed for the window at the end of the corridor, Kurt veered into the museum's high-ceilinged foyer. He was running straight for the glass front doors. Nigel was sure those doors were locked *and* equipped with loud alarms. But there was no telling Kurt that. Now that he'd been jolted from his heroic fantasy, he was hysterical!

"The monsters, the monsters!" he screamed as he ran toward the doors. "It's all true!"

"Kurt!" Nigel cried, running after the boy. Out of the corner of his eye, he saw Uriah and Laurent hesitate at the end of the corridor. They'd heard Kurt's panic attack.

Soon, they began pounding back through the gallery. They were just as eager as Nigel to shut Kurt up. Together, Nigel, Uriah, and Laurent burst into the foyer.

"What are you doing?" Nigel hissed to the shrieking Kurt. "This way!"

"Let me out!" Kurt screamed, ignoring Nigel and pounding on the glass doors. "I want out! I want to go home!"

He grabbed the door handle and twisted it desperately. But, of course, Nigel had been right. The doors were bolted shut.

So Kurt found a key . . . of sorts. He grabbed a heavy fire extinguisher from its mount next to the doors, and hurled the tank through the glass! The doors shattered with a tremendous crash.

Weee-oooooh-weeee-oooh!

That would be the alarm I was worried about, Nigel thought wearily. He hung his head in defeat.

But Uriah wasn't going down that easily. He grabbed Kurt away from the still-tinkling glass door and shook him violently.

"You goofball!" he yelled. "If we're caught, it's all your fault!"

"Let's get back to the window in the back of the museum," Laurent snarled. He dashed out of the foyer and began running back up the corridor. Uriah and Kurt followed him, with Nigel close on their heels.

As Nigel entered the long gallery and veered to his left, he dared to glance over his shoulder at the spot where the snake-man and the blue dude had appeared. Were they getting ready to chase after the boys? Were they arming themselves with snake-venom bombs? Maybe some blue fireballs? Or perhaps some other space-age weapon Nigel couldn't even conceive of?

Actually, the villains looked as though they were . . . leaving! But they weren't walking through any door. Instead, they were standing within a cyclone of strange smoke—cloudy stuff that glinted and glimmered, like phosphorescence on a tropical sea. Clearly, the smoke was some sort of magic! It must have transported the thugs into the museum. Now it was spiriting them away. The creatures began to dim and blur as the smoke coiled and undulated around them, filling their lungs and clouding their vision.

Despite his fear, Nigel found himself staring

at the swirling magic. It was mesmerizing!

It was only when he heard a gruff voice call out, "Hey! Stop where you are!" that Nigel was jolted back to the present. A security guard had finally discovered them!

Nigel turned to run after his friends. As he did, he took one last glance over his shoulder at the fading monsters. They had all but disappeared into the magical smoke. But just before they evaporated entirely, Nigel saw something else!

It was a girl.

She had long, straw-colored bangs and dark, weary circles beneath her eyes. Standing in front of the looming monsters, she looked tiny. Vulnerable. Resigned.

She also looked vaguely familiar!

But Nigel didn't have a chance to get a good look at her before she faded away. And besides—he had to make a break for it!

He joined the gang as they raced through the gallery toward the window.

"Halt!" the security guard shouted behind them.

"Don't even think about it," Uriah ordered his boys. "Get outta here. Quick! Quick!"

"Stop!" the guard bellowed once more.

And suddenly—Nigel did.

He grabbed Uriah's elbow and dragged him to a halt, too.

"Uriah," he breathed. "We have to give ourselves up. Running will just make things worse. And besides . . ."

Nigel glanced back at the security guard, who was gaining on them quickly. His mustachioed face was contorted with rage, and his right hand was resting on a black holster clipped to his belt.

"He has a gun!" Nigel added.

"So, stay here, idiot!" Uriah spat, wrenching his arm from Nigel's grip. Nigel winced as Uriah called him the very name he'd been repeating to himself ever since the monsters had crashed the boys' little museum tour.

Idiot. Idiotidiotidiot. I'm such an idiot.

Uriah grabbed Nigel's shoulders and glowered at him.

"Sure, stay here," he growled. "But know that if you say anything about the fact that *I* was here with you, you're going to end up broken! Destroyed! Is that clear?"

"I—I . . ."

Nigel couldn't answer. So Uriah merely gave Nigel one last sneer and headed for the open window. He reached it in a few quick strides and threw himself through it.

Nigel stayed put. He braced himself. Now the security guard was going to grab him and arrest him while his friends escaped. Or . . . not! Suddenly, a powerful beam of light poured through the window, and a gruff voice outside yelled, "Freeze!"

Nigel edged over to the window and peeked through it. Several policemen were edging toward his former friends, waving flashlights and getting ready to draw their guns.

"You're caught, boys," said the lead officer. "I'm Sergeant Lair. We're taking you down to the station house so you can tell us all about your little adventure here tonight. No false moves, now . . ."

A half hour later, Nigel found himself in Sergeant Lair's office. The four of them—Nigel, Laurent, Kurt, and Uriah—were lined up on a bench like crime suspects.

Not *like* suspects, Nigel realized, placing a trembling hand on his forehead, which was damp with cold sweat. We *are* suspects.

And just as it happened on TV, the boys were being treated to the "good cop, bad cop" routine. Sergeant Lair was the so-called good cop, gazing at the boys with bemused disdain.

"Monsters, huh?" he said drily. "Well, if you really want to know . . ."

Nigel held his breath hopefully. He'd seen Sergeant Lair's daughter, Irma, around school. She was a total prankster—always ready with a story or a joke. Maybe she and her dad were cut from the same cloth!

"I don't believe a word of it," Sergeant Lair finished. He crossed his arms over his barrel chest. His gray-brown hair stuck up in aggravated tufts. Everything about his demeanor said, Don't mess with me, buddy!

Uriah, of course, didn't heed this signal in the slightest. While Nigel cringed, Uriah whined, "But it's the truth, mister! They were there!"

Now the museum security guard, who'd been quietly seething in the corner of Sergeant Lair's shabby office, lunged forward.

"Your joke has gone too far," he shouted at Uriah. "You terrified everyone who was in the museum this afternoon and got yourselves into the newspaper, which is probably just what you wanted." He was clearly the bad cop.

The guard's face went purple with disgust.

"Then you got greedy," he spat. "You tried to stage a repeat performance. But things got out of control, didn't they?"

As he spoke, the guard reached behind the office desk and pulled out the sword Kurt had used to try to fend off the monsters. He also held up a painting—the fruit-filled still life. In its center, right through a rosy apricot, was an ugly, black gash.

"Hey, Frank . . ." Sergeant Lair said with a sardonic smile. "They already told you. It's the monsters who are guilty, not them!"

"Okay!" Nigel cried out, unable to contain himself any longer. "Maybe they weren't real monsters. But I can tell you for sure that we weren't alone in the museum!"

"*I'll* explain," Uriah piped up, giving Nigel an evil look. Nigel could almost see the rusty gears in Uriah's head turning, cooking up a big, fat lie for the police officers. In other words, Uriah was about to dig them an even deeper hole than the one they were already in. Luckily, the museum guard was having none of it.

"Save your breath, kid," he said. "We already heard your story. But Judge Cook, I'm sure, will be happy to listen."

With that, a crowd of adults began to parade into the room. The first was a woman in a smart, blue suit. She must have been Judge Cook. Her blue-black hair was cut in a severe bob. She had a pretty face and soft eyes. But her mouth was hardened in a disapproving frown.

Behind her were . . . everybody's parents. Kurt's mom and dad looked as hapless and hopeless as their son did. Laurent's father had his meaty arm around his distressed wife. His bushy, blond mustache twitched angrily. Uriah's parents—both of them in suits so sharp they looked as though they could slice through paper—were flanking a man with glasses and a bulging briefcase.

And finally, there was Nigel's dad. Nigel took one look at his father's stunned, sad expression and hung his head in shame.

This is what I deserve, Nigel thought. I was so stupid. So . . . selfish. I'm just glad Mom isn't here, to see her son lined up like a criminal.

She would be so disappointed.

In his brooding, Nigel was only vaguely aware of the adults' brisk proceedings.

"Are all the parents here?" Judge Cook asked. She tossed her trench coat over the back of a chair and stood behind Sergeant Lair's desk.

"Good evening, Judge," Uriah's mom said, stepping forward. She motioned with one skinny arm at the man standing next to her. "This is our lawyer. And he will tell you . . . my Uriah is innocent!"

Uriah's mom's voice grew shrill and angry.

"It was the bad influence of his friends that caused this," she shrieked. "They brought him into this scheme."

"Calm down," the lawyer whispered in the woman's ear. "Let me do the talking."

"No, sir," Judge Cook said firmly. "I will do the talking. Your little Uriah and his friends acted with complete irresponsibility tonight. It could have cost them a lot. But I don't want to put a permanent scar on anyone's record. After all, I have a daughter the same age as these boys. They actually attend the same school."

"So, are you saying they won't go to jail?"

Kurt's mom asked hopefully.

"No," Judge Cook declared, folding her arms over her chest. "Luckily, the ruined painting was just a reproduction, on display while the original was being refurbished. And I've already talked to the museum director. He's agreed to a reduced charge against the boys."

Uriah's mom flashed a thin-lipped, triumphant smile.

"What a relief!" she declared.

"But," Judge Cook said, giving the four boys a pointed look. "They're not just going to get off with a slap on the wrist, either!"

The judge had other plans for the boys.

TWELVE

"Don't be afraid," Elias told the Guardians, as he led them up a flight of stairs. They'd just completed a walk through the town to a tall, cottage with a peaked roof some distance away from the noisy main square.

Oh, right, Taranee thought with a shuddery sigh. You might as well tell me not to breathe. I've basically been nothing *but* afraid since the day I moved to Heatherfield.

Of course, back then, Taranee's fears had been pretty humdrum. She'd quaked at the idea of being a newbie at school. She'd worried about finding her way around town. She'd kept forgetting her own phone number, and she'd wondered if she'd find new friends.

Taranee almost laughed at the idea. Her

old fears, the fears of most teenage girls, were a luxury now. Today she had the fate of the world resting on her shoulders. And she was stuck inside a painting!

If Taranee only had use of her powers, she was sure she'd have felt better about this state of affairs. At first, being able to conjure fire in the palm of her hand had freaked Taranee out. She'd been sure she'd wake up one morning to find that she'd toasted her pillow like a giant marshmallow. Or worse!

But as it turned out, since she'd begun this whole Guardian thing, her fire power had gotten her out of several binds. In fact, she'd been able to rescue all her friends the last time Elyon had imprisoned them in floating bubbles in Metamoor.

Well, that was then, Taranee thought drily, and this is now. Elyon's trapped us *and* taken our powers away. We're stuck here like chickens in a coop.

"Make yourselves comfortable," Elias told the girls as he reached the top of the stairwell. One by one they emerged into a sunny art studio! Beneath the honey-colored eaves of the slanted ceiling were dozens of canvases, a palette, and a can of still-wet brushes. The air smelled of sunshine and oil paint. Taranee—who never felt more at home than in her darkroom, printing photographs—was surprised to realize that she *did* find the room comfortable.

She glanced at some of the canvases. None of them looked quite finished. They all had a pale, washed-out quality.

Elias must just be at the beginning of the process, she thought. She knew oil painting was all about piling on coat after coat of color, creating depth and light with every layer.

"I live here," Elias said, pulling off his cloak and smiling a bit sheepishly at his guests. He rubbed his slender hands together nervously. "It's not very grand, but I like it. There's an excellent view of the cathedral from this loft."

"So, you're a painter," Will said, smiling as she looked around the room.

"A painter," Elias said quietly. "If you want to call it that."

Slowly, Elias crossed the loft to a canvas propped up on an easel. A lavender cloth was draped over the painting. Gritting his teeth, Elias pulled the cloth away. Taranee leaned in for a closer look at the canvas.

Just like Elias's other paintings, this work seemed thin and hollow. The figure—a woman in an old-fashioned gown—was as shadowy as a wraith. The features of her face seemed to have been smudged away. Her fingers, folded on top of her billowing skirt, were indistinct. And the rolling hills that could be seen through a window behind her looked like nothing more than faint, green brushstrokes.

"This is all I am capable of now," Elias told the girls bitterly. "Shadows. Incomplete figures. Without my colors, I'm useless."

"But, you *do* have paint here," Cornelia noted, pointing at a few small pots of pigment next to the palette. "It's not enough?"

Elias sighed and again placed the cloth over his nonpainting.

"These works are nothing but illusions," he said bitterly. As he spoke, he kept his back to the girls. "Nothing that surrounds us really exists. That's the curse of Phobos."

Elias spun around to face the girls. His eyes looked feverish, and his lips were pale with anger.

"And now, that curse has struck you, too," he said. "What did *you* do to deserve this punishment? Did you dare to look at him? Did you approach his house?"

"Well . . ." Hay Lin said, shooting her comrades a sidelong glance. "It's sort of a long story."

Irma rolled her eyes and stepped forward.

"I'll explain it to you," she said bluntly. "We have to save the world. But Phobos and his sister don't want us to. And that's basically it."

"Oh, that's it, is it?" Cornelia said.

"Hey, I'm no poet," Irma said with a shrug. "So, sue me! I just tell it like it is."

Taranee stifled a giggle. Irma, with her cut-and-dried style, had stripped their mission of all its drama. *And* its glory.

And for diva Cornelia, Taranee thought, that just won't do!

Shooting the bickering girls a look, Will smiled at Elias.

"Actually, that's not totally it," she admitted. "We're representatives of Candracar."

"Oh!" Elias blurted out. He was looking at the girls the same way all the townspeople had looked at *him*—as if they were magical beings. "You're the legendary Guardians of the Veil! In Metamoor, your name is whispered in fear."

Elias gave the girls an appraising look. Suddenly, Taranee felt a little self-conscious about her striped tights, her turquoise wristbands, and her bouncy fronds of hair.

"For soldiers who have to save the world," Elias said carefully, "you look quite young."

"We are," Taranee admitted with a shrug. She was usually tongue-tied around grown-ups. For some reason, though, she felt comfortable being candid with Elias. "We just got our powers recently, actually."

"Powers that have gone kaput," Irma complained. She strolled over to one of the loft's tall windows, which were thrown open to let in the sweet-smelling spring breezes. "In this painting, air, water, fire, earth—they're all beyond us," she said with a big sigh.

"Yes, you can't quite get a grip on anything here," Elias explained. "You'll soon realize that you feel no hunger and no thirst. You never get sleepy. . . ."

"But," Hay Lin interrupted, "how do you know all these things? Who are you, sir?"

"I would have thought you would have figured that out by now," Elias said. He placed a mournful hand over his heart. "I'm the one who painted all this. I'm Elias Van Dahl, official portraitist of the court of Metamoor.

"At least, I was," Elias added darkly. "Until Phobos wanted me gone."

Taranee took a sudden step forward. She wanted to put a sympathetic hand on Elias's shoulder. He looked heartbroken!

It was clear, however, that any comfort Taranee and her friends could offer this thin, tortured man would fall on deaf ears. His wan eyes grew vacant as he motioned for the Guardians to sit. They lowered themselves onto cushions and tarp-covered boxes nearby. They stared at Elias with wide eyes.

He began his story.

"For a long time," he said, "I worked for Metamoor's royal family. I painted the king and queen in their coronation robes. And when the royals disappeared, I painted dark abstractions—pictures of the kingdom's grief. Then Phobos ascended to the throne."

At the mention of the evil prince's name, Elias's slender fingers curled into fists. A vein began to pulse in his pale, high forehead.

"Life in Metamoor was never easy," he admitted. "But under Phobos's rule, it was close to impossible. He was obsessed with his own power. Nobody was good enough to look upon his beautiful face. In fact, he issued a proclamation, ordering that every image of him be destroyed. The public squares and libraries of Metamoor were littered with shards of Phobos's statues and busts. Paintings were slashed. And Phobos shut himself up in his castle. The only connection he had with his people was through the murmurers—flowerlike spirits who act as Phobos's eyes and ears.

"I was just a simple court painter," Elias continued with a shrug. "But the mere ability to capture Phobos's face—a face I knew well—made me one of his enemies. I was watched at all times. One night, I felt the presence of a giant man. Actually, a half-serpent, half-man. He followed me along my walk home, hissing threats at my back. He had a giant, blue creature with him."

Taranee exchanged a wide-eyed look with Will. They knew all too well who had stalked Elias in Metamoor—Cedric and his ever-present, cobalt-colored henchman, Vathek.

That snaky jerk is *everywhere*, Taranee thought indignantly.

"The creatures meant to intimidate me," Elias said. "And it worked. I decided to leave Metamoor. I found a portal to another dimension—and another time. In fact, I made my way to your world. I found a time period where artists like me were appreciated."

"When was that?" Taranee asked bluntly. "Last time I checked, modern people like their art tucked away in museums."

"The seventeenth century, in Europe," Elias answered matter-of-factly. "I created a new identity for myself—a new life."

As Elias reminisced, two spots of color appeared on his pale, thin cheeks. His smile, for the first time since the Guardians had met him, became easy and genuine. Taranee couldn't help returning the grin.

"I was free to paint," Elias continued with a sigh. "To dream and hope. Even . . . to love."

On that last word—love—Elias's voice grew thin. He brushed the surface of one of his shadowy canvases with his fingertips. Then he let his hand fall limply to his side.

It was then that Taranee realized something. Every painting in the loft looked the same. Washed-out and shadowy though the images were, Taranee could still make out the figure of one woman. She had honey-brown hair and a pink gown. Her smile was lilting and confident. Her eyes were perhaps hazel. Or maybe they were green. The colors were too faint to tell.

But the love that Elias had poured into those works was all too vivid.

"For a very brief while," Elias said huskily, "life was sweet. But Phobos didn't forgive me for escaping. I was found by some of his henchmen—Lord Cedric and a couple of massive, blue-skinned ruffians. They surprised me in my studio, where I was painting my beloved Alexandra. His lackeys grabbed me. I can still remember Cedric's every word."

'Since you love your job so much, painter,' he said, 'it is inside one of your masterpieces that you will spend the rest of your existence!'

Of course, Cedric didn't banish me into Alexandra's portrait," Elias said with a rueful smile. "Her presence might have given me solace. Instead, he chose *The Never-Ending Spring*. The painting became a portal in the Veil. Cedric sent me through that portal, then closed the door forever. He returned to

Metamoor, and I was left to languish here in this frivolous world I had created—a world that, thanks to evil magic, suddenly came alive."

Taranee gasped and Elias fell silent for a moment. As her friends shook their heads in disbelief, Taranee craned her neck to glance out the window. She could see the townspeople milling about in the distant square. It was hard to believe they didn't really exist! Their lives played themselves out endlessly, as if on some cosmic treadmill. Meanwhile, they never experienced the pleasures of sleep, or a hot meal, or, simply, love.

Taranee gazed at Elias. Heartbreak had hollowed out his cheeks and stooped his slender shoulders.

I wonder, Taranee thought wistfully, if a boy could ever love me that completely.

Then another musing wormed its way into Taranee's mind: if, by some miracle, a boy *did* fall for her, would she be too shy, too fearful, to seize the opportunity? The thought caused a shiver of anxiety to rush through her. But then she shook her fear away. She had to focus.

Elias had resumed his story.

"This world is called *The Never-Ending Spring*," Elias pointed out, "but it really should be called *The Last Tear*. I had imagined a story behind the painting. This place was a happy village, where nobody had had reason to cry for centuries. To remind them of their luck, its people put the last tear ever shed here in a glass vial and stored it in the center of their cathedral." His voice trailed off.

Elias plodded to the window and gazed out at the town. Taranee walked over to stand next to him.

"These people are not real." He gazed down at a couple of plump teenagers scurrying down a path in front of the house. "But they live a never-ending day."

"It's a nightmare," Taranee breathed.

"It's Phobos's evil," Elias said. His voice caught in his throat. "He's forced me to stay in this painting for . . . how long has it been? . . ."

"Four hundred years, Elias," Will said gently. "We come from the twenty-first century."

"Four hundred years," Elias gasped.

"You barely look your age," Irma piped up, trying in her own way to be helpful.

"Shut up, Irma," Cornelia hissed.

Hay Lin stumbled up to one of the paintings. She squinted at the woman's washed-out smile.

"And the woman in the painting?" she asked Elias. "Alexandra?"

"I never got to say good-bye to her," Elias said. "And that is why I will never stop suffering. If only I could, at least, draw her. . . ."

Elias couldn't finish his sentence. He choked on the words, then hid his face in his thin hands. Taranee felt tears well up behind her own glasses. She sighed deeply. Elias's story was better than any romance novel. And worse, because it had really happened. The tragedy of it all was too much!

Will gave her friends a stricken look as Elias's shoulders heaved with silent sobs. When the artist finally regained his control, she stepped forward.

"Elias, we will help you to draw Alexandra," she said with determination. "I think I know how to give your colors the kick they need!"

"How?" Elias sputtered in disbelief.

"Well . . ." Will said, looking around her. Taranee tried to see the room through her friend's eyes. She saw a medieval house composed of nothing but paint and canvas. She saw five girls with wings sprouting from their backs. In short, she saw a scene that was nothing less than preposterous!

"I guess this is a silly question," Will said with a small laugh. "But do you believe in magic?"

THIRTEEN

Will and the other Guardians followed Elias across the town square. As they made their way through the throngs of revelers, the boisterous celebration stopped completely.

"Oooh!" one woman cried out, pointing at Will's wings with a fearful expression.

"There they are," a soldier said angrily.

Next to *him*, a stout man in a fuzzy, red beard glared disapprovingly at the Guardians' mod outfits.

"What impudence," he sniffed.

Wonderful, Will thought sarcastically. I always love being the center of attention.

Will became aware of her shoulders creeping up toward her ears. Her eyes widened, and her hands began to tremble. But then she

glanced at her comrades.

Cornelia was glaring at the gawkers.

Hay Lin was greeting their scrutiny with a willfully oblivious, sunny smile.

Irma, of course, was smoothing her hair and giving the crowd movie-star smiles.

That's Irma, Will thought with a small smile. She craves the limelight as much as I loathe it.

But the real point was that none of her friends were making any apologies for being there in the painting. *They* knew they weren't the enemy. In fact, when all this was over, the Guardians might very well have saved the *Never-Ending Spring*ers from the drudgery of their incessant, sunny day!

So *there*, Will thought, sticking her chin out. She relaxed her shoulders and began to stalk behind Elias with confidence.

Elias, too, was putting on a jovial face.

"Cheer up, people," he called as his colorful crew made its way across the square. "These girls are our friends. They're here to help us."

Elias glanced over his shoulder at Will. His face clouded with a sudden wave of doubt.

"At least," he whispered, "that's what you've told me."

"Well, it's just an idea I have, Elias," Will said, in a shaky voice. Doubts of her own began creeping into her mind. She'd felt so certain about this solution in Elias's loft. But the real truth was, Will had *no* idea if her scheme would work.

And Irma wasn't helping with her two cents' worth: "Yeah, and your idea almost seems too absurd to work."

Will caught her breath and gave Irma a baleful glare. Oh, *what* was she doing?

"Listen, the first thing I noticed about this place was the stillness," Will declared, thinking out loud. As they walked, Elias and the Guardians cocked their heads to listen in. Will took a deep breath and pressed on.

"We are living in a moment that never goes by," Will explained. "So I say, let's try to change the rules. Let's face off with Phobos's spell and see what happens."

Elias looked skeptical.

"But how do you expect to do that when you don't have your powers?" he asked.

"We don't need powers for this," Will declared. "Sometimes, all you need is a little creativity."

Elias stopped in his tracks.

Okay, he *totally* hates the idea, Will thought desperately. Here's the part where he gets all snarly. Or, worse—patronizing!

"Here we are," Elias said, setting his jaw with determination.

Oh. Elias had stopped because the group had reached its destination—the front steps of the majestic cathedral that loomed over the town square. Tentatively, the group walked up the stone steps and gazed up at the tall, arched, wooden doors.

"Up to now, you've used well water to mix your paints," Will pointed out to Elias.

"Yes," he nodded.

"But today, you'll use the tear stored in that vial," she declared. "A tear is a sign of sadness, yes, but also of humanity. Of a soul! Who knows—it might be just the thing to shake this town up!"

"Um," grunted Taranee, as she pushed hard on the church doors. The doors did not budge.

"The entrance is blocked," she gasped.

Naturally, Will thought with a sigh. This would be too easy if the church doors weren't locked, and we could walk right in.

But, Elias was determined!

"Hey," he called to a couple of burly men arm-wrestling nearby. "Come and help us push."

The men shrugged and lumbered to their feet. As they walked over, Elias turned to Will. His cheeks were flushed with excitement.

"A world without change," he said, "is a world without hope, wouldn't you say?"

"That's the point," Will eagerly agreed. "I mean, maybe nothing will happen. But why not try it?"

With a brisk nod, Elias lined up next to the musclemen. On the count of three, the guys crashed against the church doors with their shoulders.

The doors still didn't budge.

"Again!" Elias barked.

Thump!

"You can do it, fellas!" Irma squealed in delight, jumping up and down and pumping her fists in the air.

Thump! Crack!

The doors were starting to give! The men kept going. Before long, they had broken through.

"Success!" Hay Lin cried.

The group tumbled into the church, chattering and giggling with excitement. But a moment later, they all fell silent.

Will looked up at the towering ceiling. It was beautifully gilded, with golden flying buttresses and frescoes of cherubs and angels. Ornate chandeliers held flickering candles. At the front of the church, a giant, round, stained-glass window showered the group with warm, rainbow-colored beams.

"This is really remarkable," Irma whispered.

"Beautiful," Cornelia said, for once agreeing with Irma.

"I've always just drawn this church's exterior," Elias gasped as he stumbled down the cathedral's central aisle. "This is the first time I've seen the inside."

Will spotted an altar halfway up the aisle. It was the spot where an ordinary church would have stored a bath of holy water. Crossing her fingers, Will hurried up to the pedestal.

On top of it was a pink, silk pillow. And nesting in the pillow was a small, glass bottle plugged with a cork.

Gingerly, Will closed her fingers around the bottle. It felt dusty, but warm, as if life itself had been sleeping within the tiny vial.

This *has* to work, Will thought. She almost sobbed as she handed the bottle to Elias.

"This must be the last tear," she said. "Take it, Elias. Take it, and use it to make your paints."

As Elias stared at the tiny bottle in wonderment, Will felt a surge of pride well up in her chest. She looked up at the cathedral's ceiling and flashed a defiant smile. She hoped Cedric could see them now. She could just imagine him, seething as they defied his spell and took steps to break free of his prison.

He'd be pacing around one of his cold, stony chambers, ranting to his witless blue flunky, Vathek.

"This is impossible," he'd say. "Those girls are putting my patience to the test."

"Is there *anything* that will work on them, Lord Cedric?" Vathek would respond, wringing his fat claws anxiously.

"*Nothing's* working," Cedric would complain. "Why is everything so complicated? Used to be, when people were cast out by a spell, they stayed in their corners, meekly and quietly, until the end of their days! These girls are just so arrogant!"

Will giggled under her breath. Thwarting that snaky Cedric was totally satisfying! She dipped back into her happy fantasy.

"It's true, master," Vathek was saying sympathetically to Cedric. "Do you want me to take care of them?"

In Will's imagination, Cedric stopped his pacing.

He turned to gaze at Vathek with revenge in his icy blue eyes. A tight smile stiffened his perfect face as he shook his head. And suddenly, Will felt a prickle of fear crawl up her neck.

"No, Vathek," Cedric hissed. "Somebody else is anxious to see the Guardians. He wants a final word with them!"

Will tried to shake the fantasy—now a creepy one—out of her mind. But when she returned to reality, she found it to be, if possible, even worse!

"Mr. Van Dahl," an eerily familiar voice roared. Will spun around, looking for the voice's source. It seemed to be reverberating off every stone surface in the giant cathedral!

"I wouldn't go anywhere with that vial if I were you," the voice said.

Then something began to happen in the middle of the church aisle.

That something started as a slight warping of the air. Will's vision turned watery and wavery. No—it wasn't Will's eyes. It was the air!

A circle of silvery smoke began to appear in it. At first, the haze swirled lazily. Then, its movements accelerated. The circle began to widen. Before anyone had a chance to react, it was ten feet in diameter. Its edges crackled and roiled with evil magic.

It's—it's a portal! Will realized with a gasp.

Fwaaaammmm!

And that would be the all-too-familiar sound of somebody bursting *through* the portal, Will thought, letting out a small scream.

Thump! Thump! Thump!

"Yah!"

Suddenly, a menacing horseman—make that horse-monster!—burst through the smoky ring! His blue face was set into a predatory grin. His suit of armor clanked heavily. And his horse—which actually looked more like a swift-footed rhinoceros—blew angry jets of fiery, red steam from its nostrils.

"It's Frost the Hunter!" Will screamed.

The Guardians had run into this very evil Metamoorian dude before. They'd outwitted him. So *now*, he was hopping mad.

Maybe I *didn't* imagine that conversation between Cedric and Vathek, Will thought shakily. This is terrible!

Suddenly, however, Will realized something: If Cedric really is watching, and if he thinks this situation is dire enough to send his strongest bounty hunter, then I *must* be onto something!

Will whirled around and grabbed Elias by the shoulders.

"This proves I was right," she cried. "Elias, we can do this! We can break that spell!"

"B—but—"

Elias's eyes bulged with terror. Frost's rhino was clomping around the group threateningly. But Will didn't have time for fear.

"Do as I tell you!" she barked at the man. "Run home and mix your paints with that tear!"

Before Elias could answer, and before Will could think twice about what she was doing, she shoved Elias roughly from their midst. He missed being gored by the rhino's horn by only a few inches—but he made it.

Irma waved Elias out of the cathedral.

"Go, now!" she urged him. "We'll deal with Frost."

Elias darted out into the street. Frost let him. It was the Guardians he was after.

A fact that Cornelia found just a *bit* irksome.

"Nice, Irma," she hissed at her friend. "And *how* exactly do you think we'll deal with that beast?"

"See, that's your problem, Cornelia," Irma retorted. "You're so type A. You always have to have a *plan*! *Bo*-ring. I say we wing it."

"Not that we have much choice," Will said nervously.

Meanwhile, Frost had a plan of his own. He'd pulled his steed to a halt in front of the last tear's now empty altar. Behind him, the brilliant, stained-glass window looked like a heavenly halo.

Now *that's* a cruel joke, Will thought. But she refused to be cowed. She linked arms with her friends. Together, they glared at the villain.

"I'll be taking care of your painter friend later," Frost informed them. "Now I'm ready for you, Guardians. You've already escaped me once. But that will *never* happen again."

"I hate to contradict you," Hay Lin said chirpily. "But the door is that away!"

Hay Lin pointed behind her. Then she grinned at her girlfriends. En masse, they spun around and began to race away from Frost.

"No!" the hunter roared.

Ta-dooom! Ta-dooom! Ta-dooom!

That was the rhino's giant hooves, thundering after the girls. As Will sprinted down the aisle, she eyed the open doorway. It looked as though it were about ten feet tall.

Let's just hope this works, Will thought desperately.

To her friends, she said, "Keep going! Let him follow us!"

"Let him follow us!?" Cornelia sputtered as she sped along next to Will. "Have you *seen* that thing he's riding? He'll catch up to us in about five seconds."

"Maybe not," Will grunted.

At that moment, the five girls plunged through the doorway. They careened down the steps and darted into the square. Only then did Will allow herself to look back at their pursuer.

Whammmm!

Will saw the rhinosteed gallop through the

doorway. But Frost remained in the cathedral. More specifically, he was sprawled on the cathedral *floor*, groaning. Will's calculations had been correct. Atop his giant rhinosteed, Frost's head definitely rose ten feet into the air. As the steed slipped through the doors, Frost had banged into the doorjamb with all the force of a battering ram.

"He was too busy chasing us down to remember to duck!" Will said with a cackle. The girls watched as Frost rubbed his head and moaned woozily.

"He took himself out!" Taranee cried. "We didn't have to do anything."

"I didn't lie, did I, Frost?" Hay Lin yelled in triumph at the big, blue bully.

"Grrrrr!" the hunter roared, as he lolled weakly on the ground. "This is gonna cost you, Guardians."

Splatttt!

An answer came in the form of a rotten orange. The fruit hit Frost square in the face!

"Irma!" Will cried accusingly. "Was that really necessary?"

"But . . . it wasn't me!" Irma protested.

"No," said a voice from somewhere behind

the Guardians. "It was us!"

The girls turned to see a couple of soldiers, *and* a host of townspeople, stalking toward them through the square.

"Listen, knight," the soldier spat at Frost. "Aren't you a little old to be chasing down five young girls?"

"We don't want any trouble in our village," a brash young man declared from behind the soldier. "Why don't you go away?"

"You don't know who you're talking to," Frost grunted, lurching to his feet. Weakly, he pulled a giant sword from its sheath on his belt. "Don't go against me."

"*Maybe* you didn't understand us," the soldier yelled. "We've asked you nicely to hit the road. But if you want to do this the hard way, you need only say the word."

"It works! It *works!*"

Uh, *that's* not the word I was expecting, Will thought. She peered into the crowd for the source of the joyful outburst. Suddenly, Elias broke through the throng. He was grinning madly and waving a small scrap of canvas.

"The tear did the trick!" Elias cried. He thrust the canvas scrap at Will. The paint on the cloth was still wet, but Will could see that it was also dancing with color. The reds were vivid, the yellows, warm and nuanced. "I can paint!" Elias crowed.

Elias's joy was infectious. Will waved his picture in the air and jumped for joy. As she did, she detected an extra spring in her step.

Her arms, too, seemed more powerful.

If the tear broke the spell, she suddenly realized, then that means our powers are back!

Will closed her eyes and clenched her right fist. Almost immediately, she began to feel surges of pink magic move through her veins. The power traveled up her arm, then tunneled into her heart, her muscles, her mind.

When she opened her eyes, the Heart of Candracar—glowing and pulsing as brightly as ever—was hovering over her open palm.

"Air!" Will cried, tossing a silver teardrop of magic over to Hay Lin.

"Earth!"

Will sent a pulse of green power to Cornelia.

"Water! Fire!"

Irma and Taranee were infused with their magic, too. Hay Lin threw her arms into the air and conjured up a great gust of wind. Irma began redirecting the spray of the town square's fountain. The great gush of water headed directly for Frost.

Taranee bounced a ball of fire in her palm threateningly. And Cornelia stomped on the ground, creating a crackling fissure that began to make its way toward the increasingly cowed blue thug.

"Oh, no!" Frost cried out in panic as he watched the Guardians spring into action.

Oh . . . yeah! Will rejoiced silently. We've triumphed!

And it wasn't, she suddenly realized, just because of the Guardians' magic. She and her friends had survived this latest battle by bonding together and trusting their wits.

They were coming into their own.

And when the next battle arrives, Will thought, with fierce determination, we will be ready!

AND THIS MUST BE THE VIAL WITH THE LAST TEAR. TAKE IT, ELIAS....

... TAKE IT AND USE IT FOR YOUR COLORS!

DON'T LISTEN TO HER, ELIAS....

... I WOULDN'T DO THAT IF I WERE YOU!

IT'S FROST THE HUNTER!

FWAAAM

B—BUT...

THIS PROVES THAT I WAS RIGHT, ELIAS! WE CAN MANAGE TO BREAK THAT SPELL! GO!

DO WHAT I TOLD YOU! RUN HOME TO MIX YOUR COLORS!

GO, NOW! WE'LL TAKE CARE OF HIM!

NICE, IRMA! JUST HOW DO YOU THINK WE'LL BE ABLE TO TAKE THAT BEAST DOWN?

THAT'S YOUR PROBLEM, CORNELIA! YOU DON'T HAVE A POSITIVE ATTITUDE!

I'LL TAKE CARE OF THE PAINTER LATER! BUT I'LL FINISH YOU OFF FIRST! YOU'VE ALREADY ESCAPED FROM ME ONCE....

WE DON'T WANT TO CONTRADICT YOU, BUT WE'RE GOING TO ESCAPE THIS TIME, TOO....

KK-RAAM

NO!

OUT, QUICKLY! MAKE HIM FOLLOW US!

FASTER, CRIMSON! LET'S TAKE THEM!

LET HIM FOLLOW US? HE'S ON A HORSE! HE'LL GET US IN A MINUTE!

MAYBE NOT, CORNELIA . . .

. . . FROST IS TOO BUSY FRIGHTENING US TO REMEMBER TO LOWER HIS HEAD.

KRONG

UHHHN . . .

UH-OH . . . YOU WEREN'T EXAGGERATING!

HE TOOK HIMSELF OUT!

GRRR . . . THIS JOKE WILL COST YOU. . . .

SPLAT

!

IRMA!

BUT IT WASN'T ME!

IT WAS US, KNIGHT! AREN'T YOU A LITTLE TOO BIG TO BE ANNOYED WITH FIVE GIRLS?

!

WE DON'T WANT ANY TROUBLE IN OUR VILLAGE! WHY DON'T YOU GO AWAY?

DON'T GO AGAINST ME! YOU STILL DON'T KNOW ME. . . .

DIDN'T YOU HEAR WHAT MY SOLDIER ASKED YOU TO DO?!

HE ASKED YOU NICELY. . . . BUT IF YOU PREFER TO HEAR IT SAID WITH FORCE, YOU HAVE ONLY TO SAY THE WORD!

IT WORKS! IT WORKS!

HUH?

IT WORKS, GIRLS! THE TEAR HAS BROUGHT BACK THE COLOR. . . .

... AND WHEN YOU FINISH WAXING THE CORRIDOR, THE STEGOSAURUS IS WAITING IN THE WEST WING.

BUT, MISTER DIRECTOR ... WE ALREADY DUSTED IT YESTERDAY.

HAVEN'T YOU HEARD OF "THE DUST OF THE CENTURIES"? THAT BEAST IS MILLIONS OF YEARS OLD....

DIVIDE THAT BY A CENTURY AND YOU GET... HMMM...

HEY, HOW MANY MILLIONS OF YEARS DOES IT TAKE IF YOU DIVIDE IT BY A CENTURY?

THREE MONTHS, KURT! WHICH WE'LL BE SPENDING HERE!

DON'T COMPLAIN, URIAH. THE JUDGE WAS COOL. WE GOT OFF LIGHT.

CERTAINLY! WE'LL HAVE A LOT OF FUN DURING THE NEXT NINETY DAYS....

I'M SO MAD AT SOCIAL SERVICES.... AND JUDGE COOK, TOO!

HEY! ISN'T THAT HER DAUGHTER?

SO WHAT? SHE DIDN'T HAVE ANYHING TO DO WITH WHAT HAPPENED.

DON'T GET ALL DEFENSIVE!

HELLO...

HELLO!

CULTURAL VISIT, BEAUTIES?

NO, URIAH...

...WE'VE COME TO VISIT A FRIEND.

TO BE CONTINUED...